HOW TO BE
INVISIBLE

D1347968

TIM LOTT
HOW TO BE
INVISIBLE

WALKER
BOOKS

First published in Great Britain 2013 by Walker Books Ltd
87 Vauxhall Walk, London SE11 5HJ

2 4 6 8 10 9 7 5 3 1

Text © 2013 by Tim Lott

Cover illustration © 2013 by Daniel Mountfield

This book has been typeset in Optima

Printed and bound in Great Britain by Clays Ltd, St Ives plc

British Library Cataloguing in Publication Data:
a catalogue record for this book is
available from the British Library

ISBN 978-1-4063-2423-5

www.walker.co.uk

To all the invisible people

CHAPTER ONE

13

It was the 13th of September, 13 days after my 13th birthday, when I first learned how to be invisible.

I have never been superstitious. I've been told that the number 13 is unlucky, but to me the date was nothing more than a meaningless coincidence. My father, Melchior Nyman, taught me that people cannot resist reading meanings into coincidences. Melchior is a scientist. His mind is very logical.

According to Melchior, the significance of patterns like 13, 13, 13 is an invention of the human mind. There are no signs and there are no portents. There are no omens, good or bad.

However, my father would also insist that it was impossible for his son – or anyone else – to become invisible. So he may be wrong about coincidences as well.

Peaches, my mother, sees things differently from Melchior. She is superstitious – although she would use the word "intuitive". She would be in no doubt that my learning how to be invisible would have unpleasant consequences.

Peaches was convinced that the town we lived in,

Hedgecombe-upon-Dray, had Mystical Significance even before we moved there from London. She claimed that it was sited on ancient ley lines.

I asked her what ley lines were.

She said, "There's no point in telling you because you wouldn't believe it anyway."

If she had been anyone else, I would probably have left it at that. At the time, I was rather shy – almost pathologically unassertive at times. But with my parents I was different. I felt confident with them, so I didn't mind picking arguments. In fact, I rather enjoyed it. Inside my head I was not shy at all – I was full to bursting with opinions and feelings and thoughts. But new people made me anxious. They made me clam up and stutter and stoop. I didn't know why or what to do about it.

I nagged Peaches to tell me about ley lines, and eventually she sighed and, without looking up at me, said, "They're very ancient currents of invisible energy. Old places like monuments and megaliths and temples are all connected together by them. They are present in the earth, and in the stones and the fields. If you live on a ley line, you are very lucky, because you are surrounded by special energy. So there you are. That's what a ley line is. Is my examination over? Can I go now?"

Peaches never hid the fact that she sometimes found me irritating. That was because – with her and Melchior at least – I was always very determined to follow an argument through to its logical conclusion, which tended to lay bare the flaws in their reasoning.

"So they're there, but you can't see or detect them?" I said.

"Yes," said Peaches, in a slightly weary voice.

"So how do you know they're there at all?"

"Because you can feel them. The energy isn't the same in Hedgecombe as it is in London. It's clearer. Wilder. Purer."

"I don't get it. You can't measure ley lines, you can't detect them and you can't examine them. There's no evidence."

"*Listen,* dahlin'."

The only time Peaches ever reverts to speaking in her old voice from the American South where she was born is when she gets stressed or exasperated.

"*Listen,* dahlin', you don't have any evidence for love, do you? Show me a chunk of love on a laboratory slide. There are lots of things you can't see that are real. Put a human tear under the microscope. All you'll see is water and salt."

"There would also be a number of trace elements," I said.

"You're missing the point," she said. "A tear isn't just water and salt and trace elements. It *means* something that you can't find with experiments and science."

"It's not the same."

"Blah de blah blah. As ever, it's been deeply stimulating exchanging ideas with you. But I have to go. Things to do, people to see, windows to stare out of."

"But what about the evidence?" I asked.

"Evidence isn't everything. I have to get back to work. I have a book to write. My public won't wait. See ya later, genius."

With that she marched off to her study and her precious

book. It was the first one she had ever written and she thought it was the most important thing in the world.

I disagreed with her about ley lines. I thought evidence *was* everything – I take after Melchior rather than Peaches, and my mindset is fundamentally scientific.

Which is why discovering how to become invisible flipped my world upside down.

This is how it began. School had finished for the day, and I had nothing in particular to do. I had been living in Hedgecombe for nearly a month, and Christmas was still a way off. I was looking forward to it, but it was about all that I was looking forward to.

Up until then I had spent my life in South London, where I had attended a school for gifted and talented children. The special school was necessary because my IQ was 156, which put me in a minority of 1.2 per cent of all children. I had been quite happy there. I'd had good friends in London, and that had helped me come out of my shell a little bit.

When we moved to Hedgecombe, I had to go to a normal school. I'd felt a change come over me when I walked into that school. My shoulders hunched a bit, so I felt smaller. I had a half smile on my face a lot of the time, even though nothing was funny. I found it hard to make eye contact with the other children, and I started chewing things – my nails, pencils, the corners of notebooks. I spoke too quietly, and I mumbled half the time as if I had a speech impediment, which I didn't.

It wasn't a bad school, but I knew it would take me a while to fit in. I felt hopeful that sooner or later I would get used to it – or that it would get used to me. It wasn't really challenging me intellectually, but I didn't mind too much. I made up for the unused slack in my brain by frequenting the local bookshops. There were an awful lot of them in Hedgecombe. The place was positively world famous for it.

It was hard to understand how all those bookshops managed to turn a profit. Only a few thousand people actually lived in Hedgecombe, and they couldn't buy enough books to keep all the shops in business. There were thirty bookshops in the town and the owners didn't really mind if you spent hours in there not buying anything.

I would just wander into a shop, find a book that I liked and then settle down on the floor, or a chair if there was one, to read it. No one ever bothered me. Most of the staff were just glad to have a customer, even if that customer never actually spent any money.

This particular late-autumn Tuesday was misty. The light was fading fast. Whether or not Hedgecombe is actually situated on ley lines it *does* have a great deal of "atmosphere". This has to do with it being situated deep in a river valley at the foot of a range of mountains. As a result, dense fogs and mists often roll in from the peaks and the river, cloaking the town in vaporous swirls. They are so thick sometimes that they seem to muffle sound and render the place silent, as if it's been cut off from the rest of the world.

Sometimes it's hard to see your hand in front of your face out of doors early in the morning. Rather like a fall of snow, the fog transforms the landscape and makes everything seem strange and out of focus. Sometimes the sun pokes through and creates rainbows in the air. You never see anything like that in South London.

The town is full of winding narrow cobbled streets and alleyways. It's all higgledy-piggledy and it feels as if it's bursting with secrets, especially when the town is filled with vapour and the streets are like shadows. Many of the roads are too narrow for cars to get down, so it's also quiet and mysterious.

I was wandering alone on this particular day, with no special purpose, when I noticed a little cul-de-sac, just off a paved section that ran between two small roads in the centre of the town. I'd walked along the paved section before, and even looked in one of the bookshops – quite a boring one, specializing in nautical and military matters – but for some reason I'd never noticed the tiny passageway that stretched off past the side of the cafe there.

It really was very narrow – not much wider than a couple of wheelbarrows placed side by side – and I was surprised, when I looked down it, to see in the murky distance an old flaking sign hanging over a dusty shop front. As I got closer, I could see it was another bookshop. I couldn't imagine that anyone would be able to find this shop, and with twenty-nine other bookshops in the town, the competition alone would have made it hard to survive. A single yellow street light glowed in front of the shop, turning the mist a mustard colour.

I squeezed down the passage. (I didn't literally squeeze, but it felt that way.) I thought I would find a row of shops, but it turned out that there was only one – the bookshop under the glowing light.

It didn't seem to have a name. The board above the shop front was blank. There was just the sign which swung in the wind and simply said "Books". Only the paint on the "k" and the "s" had faded, so what it actually said was "Boo".

I noticed a bird sitting on the sign. A big black one, with a white mark roughly the shape of a figure eight on its wing. I could have sworn it was staring at me. It gave me the creeps. I picked up some pebbles and threw them at the thing. It didn't move a feather. It just kept on watching me.

There didn't appear to be any lights on in the shop so I wondered if it was closed, but when I pushed on the door, it opened easily and quietly. The big black bird was still perched on the sign, like a sentinel.

There was no one in there. All there were – obviously – were books. Books on the floor, books stacked up to the ceiling, books on shelves, books on the windowsills and blocking the windows themselves. There were so many of them that hardly any light could get into the shop at all.

There were a ridiculous number of tomes stuffed into a very cramped space – the shop floor was not much bigger than a large front room. The volumes didn't seem to be arranged in any kind of order. Most bookshops, even chaotic ones, have sections for fiction and non-fiction, and sections within those sections – crime, autobiography or whatever else there might be. Here there were just books. They were piled up, layer after layer, all of them old, most of them looking rather shabby and dusty.

It was fairly obvious why there were no customers. The place was a complete shambles. The windows were dirty and the lights did not work. It also felt very cold – colder even than outside.

I picked up some boring-looking books. A cloud of dust flew into the air, making me sneeze. The sound echoed in the silence. Still, no one emerged from the gloom to attend to me.

I was just about to walk out of the shop again when I noticed that there was a doorway to the right of the serving counter. It said "Come Downstairs – Half Price on Science Fiction and Fantasy". I was a big enthusiast of both. I was reading the first volume of George R. R. Martin's *A Song of Ice and Fire* books, *A Game of Thrones*, and I was loving it. I wanted to get a copy of the second volume in the series, *A Clash of Kings*. On impulse I decided to take up the invitation.

The stairs leading down were creaky and narrow and there was barely space to get my shoulders around the corner, but, when I finally made it through, the room was exactly like the one upstairs, only even more jumbled and cluttered. The single light bulb was very dim so the room was mostly in gloom and shadow.

It had a strange smell – like old, wet leaves. I picked up a book at random – it was some kind of junky romance called *A Kiss for the Wicked*. The cover featured a very appealing trashy blonde woman in a red bikini pointing a gun at a man in a double-breasted suit. If there were sci-fi and fantasy books, it wasn't going to be easy finding them.

I noticed yet another staircase, leading further down into the bowels of the building. This time, there was a sign saying "Sci-fi and Fantasy – 75 Per Cent Off". Apparently the price dropped the deeper you went. I picked my way to the staircase, through the books strewn all over the floor, and then made my way gingerly downstairs.

This time it was almost dark. I was certainly aware that there was a lot of clutter in there, but it wasn't even worth looking at the titles – I wouldn't have been able to see anything.

Then I nearly jumped out of my bloody socks, figuratively speaking, because a loud voice suddenly spoke from an unseen corner of the room.

"Looking for anything in particular?"

The voice was odd – rough and coarse and what Peaches would have called "common", and yet with a sort of educated lilt. It was very definitely London-sounding. It wasn't the sort of voice you usually heard in bookshops – bookshop voices were usually well-spoken and polite and rather hushed. This sounded more like the man who used to sell knives from a stall at the end of a street market we used to go to in South London. His voice was sharper than the knives he sold. It cut right through you.

I stammered a bit because the place was somewhat creepy and the man, who I still could not see properly through the gloom, made me nervous. What came out of my mouth was a sort of disjointed gobbledegook.

"No. I'm … I'm … the sign said … hello? No. Science fiction. And—"

"Fantasy," said the rough voice, cutting through my burbling. A bizarre figure strode out of the shadows.

15

He was a very peculiar-looking man. For a start, he was abnormally tall, about two metres I would guess – a giant. The ceiling of the room was very low – I could probably have touched it myself if I had stretched my arm up and taken a really good jump, but he was actually bent over at quite an acute angle trying to fit under it.

He also had a ginger moustache. *Really* ginger – quite vividly red. And it was massive – so big that it covered half his face, which was thin, greyish and wrinkled.

He noticed I was looking at it.

"Like the 'tache?" he said, grinning broadly, which seemed to extend the huge growth on his lip even more, till it almost reached his ears.

I didn't respond.

"Style they call 'the Imperial'. Gone out of fashion. Not many true devotees nowadays. Of the 'tache, I mean. Shame."

I didn't respond again. I just stared at him. I sensed myself smiling. I do this when I am particularly nervous.

"Something funny?"

"No. I'm just … no."

I dried up and tried to wipe the grin off my face. Without making eye contact, I stole another look at him. I guessed he was about sixty years old. He was wearing a loud browny-orange-check three-piece suit with the two middle buttons of the waistcoat missing. He had a chewed pencil behind his ear and a pair of spectacles with slightly tinted lenses. I couldn't imagine why he would be wearing tinted glasses when it was so dark in the shop. They were the shape of half moons.

Suddenly a fluorescent light flicked on. It was

brilliantly bright and it felt like being slapped in the face. I blinked and stumbled, knocking down an enormous pile of books. I put my hand out and caught one of them, but the rest went crashing onto the floor.

"Whoopsy," said the man.

Again, I said nothing.

"What is it?" he said, nodding towards the book in my hand.

I looked at the book I had caught. It had no words on the front and no words on the spine. On the front there was a reflective surface, bright as a mirror.

"I don't know," I said. "I just … caught it."

"Caught it?" he said. "By accident?"

We both stood there in silence.

"Why don't you open it?" he said, after what seemed like several minutes had passed. He said it in the sort of voice that isn't easy to say no to, or ignore. His head was still cricked against the ceiling. He must have been very uncomfortable indeed, but he was smiling as if he was perfectly happy.

I opened it. I looked at the title page. There was no author or publisher or anything else. Just four words.

"'How To Be Invisible'," I read, in a very quiet voice.

"Can't hear you," he said.

I coughed and tried again.

"'How To Be Invisible'," I said, this time raising my voice a couple of decibels.

"That one," he said, gazing at it, and then me, intently. He spoke gravely now, as if he was addressing a very important meeting.

I did not know what to say.

"A proper dyed-in-the-wool bona fide classic," he said, nodding meditatively.

"Have you read it?" I blurted. That was my attempt to make small talk.

"Read every book in this shop," he replied, his voice brightening. "Some of them twice. It's like my personal collection. Tell you the truth, I don't much like selling them. Not that that's too much of a problem. Not many customers, see. Lots of competition here. Place is a bit hidden away."

"Yes," I said. "I can see that."

We fell into silence again. I wanted to get out of there, but didn't want to be rude. Despite the roughness of his voice, he appeared pleased to see me. There was a weird crooked smile on his face. It wasn't unpleasant, but it did make him look a bit odd, that combined with the fact that he was crouched down all the time.

"You can have that," he said.

I looked down at the book.

"Really?" I said.

"No charge," he added.

To be honest, I didn't really want the book. It was so dusty and old, it was almost certainly boring.

He tapped his nose. Then he reached over and tapped *my* nose. Just gently, but it was weird all the same since he tapped it in exactly the place my father always tapped it when he was trying to be affectionate.

"You look like the kind of boy who needs it," he said.

I didn't know what he meant, but looking back now I can see that he was right.

It seemed a good moment to take my leave, so I turned

to go back up the crooked stairs.

"Thank you very much," I said over my shoulder as I left.

"Nice to meet a true aficionado," he said, never taking his eyes off me for a moment. He said the word "aficionado" like he was Spanish or something, with a heavy accent.

"Aficionado", incidentally, means "a fan or a passionate supporter of something".

I noticed a small insect crawling among the hairs of his moustache. You'd think I would have found that repulsive, but it was a bit cute really. Like he had made a home for a friend.

The fluorescent light flicked off, and he disappeared back into the shadows.

I made my way back up the two flights of stairs and back into the street, clutching the book. I looked up. The bloody crow, or whatever it was, hadn't moved, and it was looking at me again. It had started to rain, so I put the book in my pocket. It wasn't big, only the size of an ordinary paperback.

Then something else weird happened. The bird spoke.

I supposed, since birds don't speak, that I must have imagined the sound it made was a word. But it was astonishing how much it actually sounded like that word. The word I thought I heard the bird say was "beware".

Then, finally, the bird flew off, making great arcs with its charcoal-black wings.

CHAPTER TWO

SCIENTIFIC OBSERVATIONS ON THE ADULT WORLD

When I arrived home I went upstairs, dropped the book on my bedroom table and forgot all about it. I thought I might do some homework, but it was hard to concentrate because Peaches and Melchior were arguing. They were always arguing. You might describe it as the only pastime they truly had in common. I supposed they hadn't wanted to miss the opportunity to disagree about something while I was out of the house.

I concluded that they hadn't heard me come in. I thought about going downstairs to ask what it was they were arguing about, but they wouldn't have told me. Adults do not normally share this kind of information with their children. They think they cannot handle it. But I believe that not knowing is worse.

I couldn't make out what they were talking about, because Peaches and Melchior tended to argue in voices low enough to pretend that they were not arguing. But then one word floated out from among the jumble of syllables and whispers and exclamations. It was as if that word was lit up with neon lights and hung with ringing bells, so clear was it above the other murmurings.

That word was "divorce".

Technically, Peaches and Melchior couldn't get a divorce, because they were not actually married. Melchior had been married briefly once before, when he was twenty-one years old, and it had all ended after a year. He had vowed after that never to marry again. Anyway, he said, it was the twenty-first century – who needed a piece of paper to prove that two people loved one another? Peaches pretended that she didn't care, but I had a suspicion that she did, really. She would have been too proud to say anything, though.

But they still used the word "divorce" as a shorthand for splitting up once and for all. My parents getting divorced was my greatest fear, even greater than my second greatest, which was having to make a speech in public. According to a series of opinion polls, this is the thing that most people in Britain are most terrified of, even more than death.

When I heard the word "divorce", I started thinking about the subject, furiously and compulsively.

I wondered who I would have to live with, and who I would like to live with. I hoped that nobody would ask me to choose, because it would be impossible to make up my mind. I wondered whether Melchior would move back to London if they got divorced. He had never wanted to come to Hedgecombe in the first place.

I knew for a fact that it had been my mother's idea to move to Hedgecombe, because I had heard an argument between them shortly before we left London. I heard it through their bedroom door on a Sunday at the end of summer. It had gone something like this.

"I understand what you're saying, Marie-France," Melchior said. "You've repeated it enough times. What worries me is the effect that all this is going to have on our son."

My mother's real name is Marie-France. We only call her Peaches because it's her nickname from back in America where she was born – at the Peachtree Plaza Hotel in Atlanta, Georgia, on 17 February 1974. Her mother was a cleaner there. She was born Marie-France Decoudraux. Her family were originally Creoles from New Orleans.

Then Peaches interrupted Melchior. She interrupts people frequently, especially when they're about to make a good point.

"You should have thought of that before. What about the effect on me? Have you considered that at all? You always get your own way. We've been living in this tiny house for ten years, all because of you. It's all about you, isn't it? You, you, you. I don't even like London. I never have. It's too big and it stinks. We could get a huge place elsewhere, with a garden and chickens and fresh air. I could have some space and quiet at last to finish my book. But you don't care about my book. All you care about is your experiments."

"That's unfair," said Melchior. "It's just that Strato—"

Strato is me. Strato Nyman. I was named after a Greek philosopher of science, Strato of Lampsacus, who Melchior is a particular aficionado of. Or perhaps my parents didn't want me to be the only one in the family without a totally random name.

Peaches interrupted Melchior again.

"Now we're going to have a real-life experiment, Melchior. It's called 'moving house'. It's called 'leaving London'. It's called 'living in the countryside'. Anyway, I don't care what you think – not any more. It's all decided. There's no point in talking about it."

At that point, Melchior took a very deep breath.

"But what about Strato? He'll have to leave his school and his friends. Whatever I've done – and I'm truly, truly sorry that I—"

"It's too late to say you're sorry. Don't try and say you're sorry."

"To tell you the truth, I'm sick of apologizing anyway. But can we just talk about Strato? Just for a moment?"

"Strato's on your conscience, not mine," replied Peaches. "A change will do him good. Being stuck at that special school with all those weirdos is not doing him any favours."

"They're not weirdos. Neither is Strato."

"Putting him in an ordinary school might help him develop his social skills," Peaches continued. "He's far too shy. And it would be nice if he could run around in the open, in fields and woods, among the trees and flowers."

"Strato doesn't like running. And he doesn't like trees. Or flowers. Or chickens."

"He'd better learn to, then."

"How can you be so … negligent?" asked Melchior.

"Negligent", incidentally, means "neglectful" or "careless".

"I'm *not* negligent," retorted Peaches. "No one loves

Strato more than I do. Certainly not you, standing there on your moral high ground looking down your big nose at me."

Melchior doesn't have a big nose. It is more what I would describe as "Roman". A formidable nose, I would term it. Noble.

Peaches, still in full flood, continued.

"If you were so moral, you wouldn't have – well, let's not go there. Not again. I want the best for him. I just don't think the best for him is us staying here – especially since, if we do stay here, there almost certainly isn't going to *be* an us."

Then they had gone quiet and I slipped away in case they came out and caught me listening in.

Self-evidently, Peaches had won the argument, because we moved to Hedgecombe not long afterwards.

She usually does win arguments. She is very good at them.

I did like trees and flowers, whatever Melchior said. I just thought they were a bit boring compared with computers and books and physics. I didn't much like chickens though. But I thought I could get used to them.

I hadn't so much been worried about leaving London as saddened that Melchior had to leave his job and move to a smaller, less prestigious establishment. In London he had been at the heart of his field, surrounded by the most up-to-date, state-of-the-art equipment.

He had even worked on dark matter projects. He had been very highly valued in the scientific community. I wasn't sure what he was doing after we moved to Hedgecombe. I was sure that it was pretty important though. All the same, I knew we had less money. We'd had to sell the car and buy an older one, Peaches did all her shopping in sales and charity shops instead of posh boutiques, and Melchior had started buying a much cheaper brand of whisky for himself.

It didn't help that Peaches' job as a part-time writer – by "part-time" I mean "unpublished" – meant there wasn't much money coming in on her side, although her friend Dorothea Beckwith-Hinds, who worked in publishing, had apparently offered her some kind of deal for her first book. Peaches was now absolutely obsessed with finishing it and didn't believe she could do it anywhere but in a remote part of the countryside.

She wouldn't tell me what the book was about. But when I learned how to be invisible, I found out the secret.

Only I wish sometimes that I hadn't.

However bad that particular argument in London had been, this one was worse, because they used the D-word. The thoughts started to chase one another around my head. If I stayed with Peaches, and Melchior moved to London, would I have to travel back and forth between them on the train by myself? And who would cook for me if I ended up living with Melchior? He is a bloody terrible cook – his spaghetti bolognese is the worst I have ever tasted. Most of all, was it my fault? And if it was, what had I done wrong?

The word "divorce" continued sliding painfully around my head like a handful of tin tacks. I didn't like it. I hoped that hearing the word didn't mean what I thought it might. I could still hear Peaches and Melchior going at it downstairs. Their rows could be very protracted. The record was 48 minutes.

Exact measurement is very important when you are trying to calculate things scientifically, and sometimes I undertook research on Peaches' and Melchior's rows. The average length of a row was 17.3 minutes, the average intensity 3.5 on a scale of 1–5. This particular argument was about a 4 or even a 4.5.

Just to distract myself, I put down my homework and picked up the book that the weird gigantic man with the ginger whiskers had given me. I studied the reflective panel on the jacket. I held it up to my face. It was peculiar how the whole of my face seemed to fit in it, even close up, though it was very small. This was counter-intuitive. And the image was so clear – it was like a genuine glass mirror instead of what it must have been, perhaps some variety of tinfoil.

I turned to the page after the title page. There was nothing on it. I turned to the next page. Nothing. The one after that was the same. It turned out, in fact, that there were no words at all in the book except those on the title page: "How To Be Invisible".

It struck me as peculiar, to put it mildly. Why had the strange, stooping man in the shop recommended a book to me that only had four words in it? Why would he want to pretend it was a "classic" and then give it to me for free? What sort of book was printed with only a title page? Was it some kind of arcane bibliophilic joke?

A "bibliophile", incidentally, is "someone who loves books".

The noise from downstairs was getting louder. It was reaching a force 5 argument on the Strato Nyman Scale, a level of intensity that I have only come across once or twice. I tried to concentrate on the book – not that there was anything in particular to concentrate on. Not only no words, but no page numbers, no acknowledgements, no copyright notice. The paper itself was thick and yellowish, and it had a very distinctive smell – something like walnuts. But the tract was obviously worthless. I decided to get rid of it.

I took very careful aim at the litter bin in the corner of my room, which is just next to the full-length mirror by my wardrobe, a good three metres away, and threw the book in a looping arc. It just caught the lip of the bin, teetered and then fell the wrong way, open, onto the floor. I sighed and made my way over to it.

It was only when I bent down to pick it up, ready to drop it in the bin, that I noticed the reflection of the open book in the mirror. It was then that I realized I'd been wrong. I obviously hadn't checked all the pages. There was some writing in it after all. I could see it quite clearly in the mirror.

I picked up the book, curious now to see what it said. A book with only one page of story printed in it was in some ways even more peculiar than a book with none at all.

But when I looked at the page there was nothing there.

Once I'd got over my puzzlement, I did what any scientifically minded person would do. I decided to repeat the experiment in order to confirm my observations.

I placed the book back in front of the mirror once more. Sure enough, the words appeared again. I was too far away to read them properly – they were in quite small type – so I had to get down on my knees and put the book right up close to the glass.

There was something else odd about the words. They appeared the right way around in their reflection. Which meant that if the words really were on the page and somehow only readable in a mirror, they were printed the wrong way around.

It was most peculiar. I thought I had made an astonishing discovery that Melchior would be absolutely fascinated by. I was sure he would be able to explain it – my father can explain more or less anything – but this would challenge even his formidable intellectual faculties. Perhaps he would have to take the book to his laboratory and perform experiments on it. Perhaps he would even take me with him – something he never did, always fobbing me off by saying that I would find it "boring".

I squinted at the letters. They kept swimming in and out of view – I didn't know if there was something wrong with the book, or something wrong with the mirror, or something wrong with my eyes. The print was faded and the typeface was a bit strange – rather wiggly and old-fashioned. Gradually I began to make the words out. Not that I was very much the wiser after I had.

I copied it down, just so I could remember what it said – the letters in the mirror seemed shaky and unstable, like the pictures on a faulty television set, and I feared they might disappear. Here it is, word for word:

> *To you who remain under the shadow of nonage*
> *That which matters*
> *Is not of matter made.*
> *Words hide paper.*
> *Paper conceals space.*
> *All is emptiness.*
> *And all things forever*
> *From that emptiness*
> *Spring.*

I couldn't make any sense of it.

I turned the page – nothing. And then nothing, and nothing and nothing. This was the only page on which anything was written and … as I looked, that page also became blank. The words just disappeared in front of my eyes.

At that moment, the door opened and I dropped the book. My mother was standing there. She had a funny look on her face. Her eyes were red as if she had been crying.

"Strato," she said. "Come downstairs, please. Your father and I want to talk to you."

I forgot about the book then. I went downstairs and sat on the sofa, and my mother and father sat down opposite me. They seemed very grave and upset. I was sure they were about to tell me that they were going to separate.

Then my father said, "Is there something you want to tell us?"

I said, "I don't think so."

Then Peaches said, "Are you sure?"

And I said, "What's this about?"

Then my mother and father looked at each other, and my father looked at me with his pained, troubled, watery-blue eyes, and said, "Strato. We know that you have been playing truant."

I didn't say anything.

"We're not angry with you," said Peaches.

"We just want you to tell us why," said Melchior.

I remained silent.

"Is it because you are unhappy at school?" said Peaches.

I shook my head.

"Is it because you don't like it here in Hedgecombe?" asked Melchior – somewhat hopefully, I thought.

But I shook my head again.

"What is it then?" said Peaches.

I refused to say anything. Eventually, this annoyed them, so they sent me to bed and made me keep the light off as a punishment. So I couldn't investigate the curious matter of my new book any further. Instead I stared at the ceiling for a long time, watching spots form in front of my eyes, and wondering where they came from.

Then after about two hours and ten minutes, I fell asleep.

CHAPTER THREE

THE MYSTERY
OF THE MAGIC ATOM

I chose not to tell Melchior or Peaches the reason I was truanting because I couldn't see the point and I didn't want them to worry about me.

I was sure they felt guilty about taking me away from London, and I didn't want them to feel any worse than they probably already did. They seemed to have a lot on their minds anyway. Peaches would lock herself away in her room for hours on end, writing her mysterious book, and Melchior was spending more and more time in the research lab. They seemed not to have any time to talk to one another, let alone to me.

But the reason I was playing truant was, as they had suspected, because I didn't like my new school, White-cross Court Academy.

The reason I didn't like my school was that I was being bullied by a boy called Lloyd Archibald Turnbull, a red-faced boy with short, heavily gelled hair and a left arm that had been damaged in a car accident and which he was unable to use.

He had started making my life difficult as soon as I

arrived at Whitecross Court. Until the day when I learned how to be invisible, I had no idea what I could do about it.

I suppose I have to admit I was prime meat for a bully. I was an outsider. I was from London. I had a silly name. I was shy, which some people interpret as being arrogant or aloof.

On top of all that, I was black. I *am* black. That is to say, I have skin that is conventionally described as "black" even though in actual fact it is dark brown.

I'm not culturally black. Other black children in London sometimes called me a "coconut": black on the outside and white on the inside. My parents don't eat West Indian food. I don't listen to music by black people any more often than any other kind of music. I don't use black street slang either (though a lot of white kids I knew in London did). The only thing "black" about me is that I just happen to have skin that is darker than that of Caucasians.

"Caucasian", incidentally, is a technical term for "white people".

I prefer the word "Caucasian" to "white" because, obviously, white people aren't actually white – their skin doesn't reflect all colours of the spectrum – any more than "black" people are actually black – their skin doesn't absorb all colours of the spectrum.

Peaches is "black" too, but you can hardly tell at all from the way she looks, since her skin is almost the same colour as my father's, and he is just an everyday English Caucasian. The term other black people used to describe her skin in the old country – that's what she calls the United States – was "high yeller". She straightens her hair, so that conceals her ethnicity even more.

But my skin is dark enough for some people think I am going to assault them just because I happen to have my hood up, and my nostrils are slightly flared and I have somewhat nappy hair.

I just wanted to be who I was. I just felt ordinary. Or I had done until I came to Hedgecombe.

Being ordinary stopped being possible as soon as we came to live here, partly because I appeared to be the only black child in the town whereas in South London everyone was mixed up together – black, Asian, Chinese, Middle Eastern, you name it.

As a consequence, people here sometimes looked at me in a peculiar manner when I walked into a shop or when I was out with my mother and father. It was as if they believed I was adopted, or had somehow forcibly abducted my parents.

Peaches really is my blood mother. She is very pretty, with eyes the size and colour of pale-purple grapes. She stands very tall, and has a puzzled, quizzical expression much of the time, as if she is trying to work something important out. My father sometimes says she's "away with the fairies" and I think I know what this means. I think this means that she's a flake.

Bullies can be quite clever. Not all of them – the ones that just smack you round the head because they don't like the look of your face are not clever at all. But Lloyd Archibald Turnbull had a special talent for bullying.

I had never seen him hit anybody – although he was easily capable of it since he had built up his good arm to the extent that it was taut and muscled like a weight-lifter's and could clearly pack a hefty punch.

If you were not watching closely you might think that he was not a bully at all. He had a nice face really – open, with a slight smile always playing at the edge of his lips, and bright blue eyes set above cheeks as red as crab apples. But maybe faces can't really tell you much about the way people are. Shakespeare said that "one may smile, and smile, and be a villain", and he knew what he was talking about.

This is an example of the way Lloyd Archibald Turnbull operated. Three days after starting at Whitecross Court, I had been sitting down to school lunch. The food was vegetarian lasagne, which was of indifferent quality but edible enough, although a little heavy on the salt. (I try to stay health conscious, and sodium chloride, over a lifetime, can raise your blood pressure to hazardous levels.)

I was sitting on my own. I didn't mind. I am the sort of person who quite likes his own company and nobody knew me yet, so why should they want to sit with me? I wouldn't have wanted to if I'd been there for some time and somebody new suddenly arrived. I would have expected a newcomer to try and fit in and bide their time until people got used to them.

That was what I'd been doing that lunchtime – biding my time, quite happily sitting there reading my copy of A Game of Thrones. I was loving it. It was better even than The Lord of the Rings, my previous all-time favourite book. It was more grown up – full of real full-on violence and also quite sexy.

From time to time I tentatively glanced up at the other children, who more or less ignored me except for one girl of about my age with round pink-rimmed glasses, shiny black hair, translucent skin and a mole on her neck. She caught my eye for a moment, then looked away again.

Lloyd Archibald Turnbull was sitting with some friends at the next table. I knew who he was because he was in my class and he often got himself into trouble by misbehaving. To my great surprise, he gestured as if to call me over. Then he called out. Nothing rude, just my name, "Strato – hey, Strato." Although I would just as soon have sat by myself, I didn't want to be impolite, so I went rather nervously over to join him.

Lloyd Turnbull didn't say anything. He just waved for me to sit down on the only empty chair. The other chairs around him were occupied by his friends, who were all talking loudly and laughing with one another. I didn't know their names, but I sat down with them just as he had requested.

I tried not to look at his damaged arm, which was not actually that spectacular, just a little skinny and slack-looking. I had heard that his nerves had been damaged in the car accident, but that there was hope they could be repaired in the not too distant future, since medical technology was moving so fast. His other arm – the big one, cabled with veins and sculpted with muscles – was much more interesting, since it was so out of proportion to the one on the other side of his body.

I'd imagined that, as he'd asked me over, he would talk to me. But, on the contrary – he completely ignored me. So did everyone else at the table. I just sat there, while he and his friends carried on talking about all the things they were doing and the people they knew, grinning as if to ingratiate myself. Frankly, it was humiliating.

Sometimes I do that stupid *Star Trek* thing in my head. When I don't want to be somewhere, I think to myself, *Beam me up, Scotty.* That's what Captain Kirk used to say to the chief engineer of the Starship Enterprise, Montgomery Scott, when he was in a tight spot and wanted to escape. Scotty would then teleport Captain Kirk back to safety, unless the equipment wasn't working or was overloaded or being sabotaged by Klingons, which it frequently was.

My dad always used to use the phrase when he was a kid – he's so old he used to watch the original TV series – and he still says it sometimes. It just kind of seeped into my mind and I can't seem to get out of the habit of using it. And that's what I'd thought when I was sitting with Lloyd Archibald Turnbull and his friends.

When lunch was over, they all just got up and went away without a word. None of them had said anything to me at all, the whole time. It made me feel very stupid and embarrassed. But Lloyd Archibald Turnbull had smiled and waved as they left the table, as if it had been the most normal and friendly thing to do to invite me over.

That's the sort of thing he did – he pretended to be friendly, so you dropped your defences, and then he showed you up in some way or other or made you feel silly.

*

The morning after Peaches and Melchior discovered that I was truanting, I headed out to Whitecross Court to face my first day back at school that week.

I took the bus as usual. I caught the same bus at the same time every day, with the same driver. His name was Mr Maurice Bailey.

The provision of public transport in Hedgecombe is quite different from London. In the metropolis, you would never know the bus driver's name, and he, or she, would conventionally display the signs of being acutely unhappy, to the point of being clinically depressed.

In London, if you were running for the bus, I swear most bus drivers positively derived pleasure from waiting until you had almost got to the stop and then pulling away, leaving you on the pavement. It was as if their job description required them to be sour and mean-spirited.

Mr Maurice Bailey wasn't like that. Everybody knew his name and called him by it. He knew all the children's names too. He was very friendly and cheerful, and didn't seem like he was about to commit suicide like the drivers in London. He had bulgy cheeks, a crinkly neck and a thin layer of hair that he combed over the top of his head. He always wore a tie and a neatly pressed shirt. If you were late for the bus and he saw you running for it in the mirror, he'd wait for you and smile at you when you came on board.

He was, nevertheless, somewhat odd in his habits and his appearance. Mr Bailey wore clothes that were always a bit too small for him – or perhaps he had simply grown out of them, since he was rather on the fat side. Also, when he wasn't driving the bus, he was famous for driving around town in an old British Army World War II Land Rover that was noisy, rusting and pumped out great black clouds of lead-filled fumes into the air. Many of the locals objected to it, claiming it was an eyesore and an environmental hazard, but Mr Bailey practically lived for the thing. At weekends, he could be seen polishing it, or underneath it fixing up some piece of machinery that had failed or was falling off (it was always breaking down).

Mr Bailey also behaved strangely towards me in a way that London bus drivers hadn't. He asked me peculiar questions like, "Where you from then?" And when I told him that I was from London he would say, "Where you *really* from though?" I didn't know what to say. I'm really from London.

When I got to school, I tried to avoid Lloyd Archibald Turnbull, but at break time he saw me sitting in the playground reading the George R. R. Martin book. He came over and, friendly as anything, started talking to me.

"Hello, Strato," he said.

"Hello," I replied, trying to cloak my anxiety.

"What's that you've got there?" he asked.

I held up the book so he could inspect the cover.

"What's that about?" he persisted.

I couldn't quite find the words to explain it. When I spoke, it all came out as a burble.

"It's a bit like *The Lord of the Rings*. Only without the magic. Except there is magic. But not much. And it's quite violent. Swords and battles and kings."

Then I dried up. He nodded, as if he understood completely.

"Do you think I could borrow it?" he said, to my surprise.

"When I've finished it, do you mean?" I said.

"No, I mean now."

He smiled. It seemed like a genuine smile as well.

"Well…" I said.

"I just want to have a look," he said, "and then I'll give it right back."

I hesitated. I should have realized by now that he wasn't being friendly, but I was rather hoping that maybe he really did like books – from what I'd seen in the classroom he seemed cleverer than the average child – and again, I didn't want to be rude. So in the end, I handed it over.

"Thanks," he said, cheerfully. "Nice of you."

Then as he was walking off, he said, "Strato. I'm very grateful. I'll take good care of it."

Then I watched him as he walked over to join his friends – the same ones that he had been sitting with at the lunch table that day just after I'd started at Whitecross.

When he got there, he just dropped the book in a litter bin.

His friends laughed and stared in my direction. I couldn't bear to look at them and I went to a different part of the playground.

Beam me up, Scotty.

Why was Lloyd Archibald Turnbull bullying me? One possibility was that losing the use of his arm in the crash had made him bitter, and he was taking it out on other children – or maybe he was showing that he could still be as tough as everybody else.

But then it might just have been me. Because there was yet another reason I didn't fit in with the crowd at Whitecross: I was a bit of a geek. To be specific, a science geek.

Most teenagers have favourite singers or favourite films, whereas I have favourite experiments. I know that must sound peculiar. After all, what's exciting about an experiment? But they can be more amazing and more surprising than anything made up.

The best example I can think of is the "double-slit experiment". It is a superdull name for what is actually a fascinating phenomenon. (Scientists like to keep things superdull because they're frightened that, if they don't, other scientists won't take them seriously.) So, for the purposes of this explanation, I will call it the "Mystery of the Magic Atom Experiment". It's very famous in scientific circles. All the explanations of it I've read make it seem quite complicated, but it's actually simple – simple to explain but hard to believe.

This is what happens.

The Mystery of the Magic Atom Experiment is performed by shooting atoms at a screen. Atoms are nothing more than tiny particles of matter, very small bits of *stuff*.(Although they're actually mainly made of empty space, but that's another story.) Scientists have invented an atom gun, just like in a science fiction novel, only real. This atom gun can fire atoms one at a time – slowly, like a pistol, or quickly, like a machine gun.

Now try to imagine the atom gun – a gun that can fire atoms one at a time. In your head, make it look like a real gun – a revolver, a cannon, a Kalashnikov, a Thompson sub-machine gun, whatever feels right.

Then imagine the mouth of that atom gun pointed at a wall (they don't *really* use a wall, but the principle is exactly the same).

If you fire a pistol at a wall, the bullet will leave a bullet hole – so you will know exactly where the bullet struck the wall.

If you fire a single atom from the atom gun at a wall, the atom will strike the wall just like a bullet would if you were using a normal pistol.

Scientists have a device that can detect exactly where the atom strikes the wall. It leaves an "atom hole" rather than a bullet hole, but it's just as real and obvious and easy to detect.

What happens in the Mystery of the Magic Atom Experiment is that the scientists put a bullet-proof (or in this case, atom-proof) screen *in between* the atom gun and the wall.

Cut into the middle of this screen there is a single slit, like an arrow slit in a castle wall – a long, thin hole.

The scientists point the atom gun in the direction of the screen (and the wall behind it), put it on to machine-gun setting, and…

BAMABAMABAMA

…let fly, spraying atoms in the direction of the screen with the slit in it and the wall.

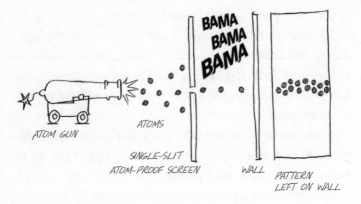

ATOM GUN

ATOMS

SINGLE-SLIT
ATOM-PROOF SCREEN

WALL

PATTERN
LEFT ON WALL

When the scientists have finished, they walk around the screen and look at the wall to see where the atoms have hit it.

Since the only atoms to have made it as far as the wall would have had to travel through the slit (all the rest would bounce off the screen, ricocheting back in the direction of the atom gun), the scientists predictably discover that the atoms that got through the hole left a slit-shaped pattern in the wall behind the screen – a mirror image of the slit, punched out in atom holes.

That's exactly what you would expect. Things only start to get weird when you create a *second* slit in the screen between the atom gun and the wall.

So now imagine two slits in the middle of the screen, both the same size and shape, a few centimetres apart.

When the scientists load up the atom gun again, point it at the screen and wall and fire it once more…

...something *entirely impossible* happens.

You know what? I think I'll come back to this later.

I'm not trying to tease anyone. I'm just beginning to realize that even explaining something very simple can take a long time in science. It's just that sort of subject.

But what the Mystery of the Magic Atom Experiment really tells you – when I get round to explaining it properly – is that one thing can be two things at the same time. Which doesn't make sense. But then a lot of the universe is like that. And everyday life, too.

CHAPTER FOUR

I THINK I'M GOING BLOODY MENTAL

When I finally got home, I decided to investigate my Facebook page. I like to play Scrabble and chess on it, and keep in touch with some of my old friends from my school in London.

There were no messages from my old school friends, but there was a request from Lloyd Archibald Turnbull to be my friend.

I was still ready to be convinced that he was being sincere. Perhaps that's why I was so attractive to bullies. Because I was willing to take people on trust.

I didn't want to stop trusting people. Then you become paranoid, and you end up twisted and bitter. Melchior always said you have to keep trusting people, even though they let you down, because a life without trust is a life only half lived. I believed he was right, but it's very hard to keep trusting people when they use it against you.

I didn't want to offend Lloyd Archibald Turnbull by ignoring his request. Another possible theoretical model to explain his inconsistent behaviour was that he was acknowledging that he had behaved badly and he now wanted to make amends. There were some other people asking to be my friend, too. I didn't know them, but I said yes to them as well. I supposed they might be friends of Lloyd Archibald Turnbull's.

One of them was the girl that I had seen looking at me in an odd way at the dinner table when I first started at the school – the one with the translucent skin and black hair and round pink-rimmed spectacles. I clicked on her page, and it turned out that her name was Susan, which was vaguely disappointing. She looked more exotic than a Susan. Susan Julia Brown. Names don't come more unexotic than that. But it was nice that she had got in touch, anyway.

Having briefly examined my cadre of new friends – Lloyd Turnbull, Susan Brown, and two boys both called Wayne, Wayne Fleet and Wayne Collingham – I decided to start my homework. But I found it very difficult to concentrate.

I tried to make a list of some Christmas presents I might like so I could give Melchior and Peaches plenty of time to shop around. I was hoping for a telescope or an iPod, and possibly a decent bike and the second volume of the George R. R. Martin series. Then I ran out of ideas.

I don't know why I had been putting it off, but it was then that I picked up the *How To Be Invisible* book again. Of course I hadn't forgotten about it. But somehow it had unnerved me, because what I had seen the previous evening was impossible, and impossible things are frightening.

I still could not figure out why the book was behaving in such a strange way (if books can be said to "behave"). What I had seen – words on a page only appearing when reflected in a mirror – made no sense. Perhaps the stress of the move to Hedgecombe was giving me hallucinations.

I decided I would check one more time, to make sure I hadn't completely lost my faculties, and then – if I had indeed observed the book accurately – show it to Melchior so that he could assess the book's unusual properties. It might prove to be one of the most exciting discoveries of all time, and Melchior would become famous and we would have plenty of money and then all our troubles would be over.

I picked the book up and flicked through it. The pages were still blank. It was scientifically impossible that they would not still be blank when I held them up to a mirror, of course. I started to consider the possibility that I was not merely imagining things – that I was, in fact, mentally ill.

Children who attend special schools, like I had, register unusually high rates of psychological disorder. I had a genius uncle who believed that starlings were flying spiders. He threw himself out of a second-floor window after watching *Peter Pan*, thinking that if he really believed it enough, he would be able to fly. He broke his leg.

That's what happens when you think unscientifically.

I very cautiously held the pages up to the mirror again. I was almost relieved to see that there was still nothing there. At least, there was nothing at all on the first page after the title page, whereas before there had been all that stuff about the "shadow of nonage" – whatever "nonage" was – and "That which matters is not of matter made". Clearly I had been letting things get to me, but now it seemed I had recovered my wits. The page remained resolutely blank no matter how many different angles I held it up at in front of the glass. Apparently I wasn't mentally unstable after all.

I was about to throw the book away – properly away, in the outside bin so that when the rubbish truck came the next day it would be got rid of once and for all – when, on impulse, I decided to turn the page. And there they were again – words, reflected in the mirror, the right way around.

I felt a giddy sensation in my stomach, but also a tangible rush of excitement. Something impossible was happening – again. But then, the way I figured it, impossible things were perfectly possible. Because although science always thinks it's so matter of fact, it's anything but. Incomprehensible things happen routinely. Thinking, for instance, about the Mystery of the Magic Atom Experiment made me think that the invisibility book might not be so impossible after all.

Whether the book was impossible or not, the words that I could see in the mirror were definitely there – although once again they were flickering and faint.

I copied them out on a scrap of paper in case they disappeared. This is what they said:

Everything is space, within and without.
The mirror is a wall that reflects all your doubt.

Run through that wall without any fear
For all that is solid will soon disappear.
Hold these words pressed hard to your heart.
The seen and unseen must surely part.

I didn't understand. I hated poems anyway – they never made any sense, and this one was no exception. My mother was always trying to get me to read poems and "proper books" instead of what she calls "trashy science fiction". But although you can lead a horse to water, you cannot make it bloody well drink.

Just as I was staring at the words, trying to figure out what they meant, there was a knock on the door. It was probably Melchior. Peaches never knocked, she just barged right in without a word.

But when I opened the door, it was Peaches after all. Unusually for her, she wasn't wearing any make-up. Her face looked tense and strained. I thought that she'd been crying. She tried to smile as if she was happy, but that's just one of the ways in which grown-ups lie.

Without speaking, she went over to the chair next to my bed. She moved the big jumble of books off it and put them on the floor, which was covered with the previous day's – and the day before's – dirty clothes. Normally she would spend between thirty seconds and one minute going on about this and telling me that she was sick and tired of having to clear up after me, et cetera, but this time she made no comment.

Somehow I already had a suspicion of what she was going to say. As I expected, she lied about it.

"Dahlin', I've got something very important to tell you."

I said nothing.

"I suppose you've noticed that your father and I haven't been getting on all that well lately. All has not been sweetness and light."

I suddenly had a clenched-fist feeling in my stomach.

"I don't know how to say this, so I'm just going to come right out and say it. Your father has decided he needs a bit of a break."

"What kind of a break?" I said, haltingly. "Like a holiday?"

I was playing dumb, but I knew what she meant.

"Not like a holiday, no. More like – well, a space in which he can think and find a little air."

"Isn't there enough air here?"

"Don't be obtuse, dahlin'. This isn't easy for me."

"Where is Dad?"

"He's just gone out for a while. He'll be back soon. I think he's a bit upset."

"So what are you saying?"

"Well, he – *we* – were just thinking about him moving somewhere nearby for a little while, just until he sorts himself out."

There was a long silence.

"How do you feel about that, dahlin'? I know it must come as a shock, but it might be better for all of us – at least in the short term. I'm sorry. I'm sure everything is going to be alright in the end, but we have to be practical, don't you agree?"

"Will he be here for Christmas?"

"Of course he will."

"I still don't understand. Why does he need more air?"

She tried to give me a hug, but I kept my hands very firmly by my sides. I realized that my hands were clenched into little fists. I looked at them. The knuckles were all white.

I wanted to ask her what I had done to make Melchior want a bit of a break from *me,* but I knew she would just pretend that it had nothing to do with me. I wanted to ask her how the hell I was *meant* to feel about it, other than furious, sad and confused. But I found it hard to say those kinds of things straight out.

Instead I just said this: "Are you going to divorce?"

She pretended to look surprised, but I knew she couldn't have been, because I'd heard her use the word "divorce" only the day before, so they must have talked about it. And now if Melchior was moving out, then they must actually be doing something about it, only of course they wouldn't be straight with me because it might upset me.

It would have been hilarious if it hadn't been so bloody sad.

"Of course we're not going to get divorced. For a start, we're not even married."

This infuriated me. Did she think I was a bloody idiot?

"You know what I mean," I said.

"I'm sure it won't come to that. You know that your father and I love you very much."

I could hardly hear what she was saying because I felt like my head was about to explode with the blood pumping through it, and I thought my fingernails were going to cut into my hands, I was clenching them so tightly.

Just then, the phone downstairs began to ring, and

Mum got this expression on her face that made her look very relieved, and she said that she had to go downstairs and answer it. It was as if she could hardly wait to get out of the room.

"I'm sorry, dahlin'. I've got to take that. I think it's about my book. I really do think it's going to be published. Isn't that wonderful?"

"Yes."

"I'm sure everything is going to be OK. When your father gets back, he'll talk to you about everything. I know it must be very confusing for you."

Then she went to answer the phone, a little too quickly, leaving me to my own devices.

I imagine that when adults hurt their children it is as if they are hurting themselves and they want to get it over as quickly as possible.

I did not expect her to come back any time soon. I had no doubt that the urgent phone call was going to take plenty of time. As for Melchior, where was he? It would have been nice if they could have sat down with me together and told me what was going on. It made me feel very angry.

On the other hand, I was rather glad he hadn't been there in a way – my father is even worse than my mother at talking about things that are "difficult", though I didn't know what was so difficult about telling the truth.

I sat down on the chair where Peaches had been sitting. It was still warm from her body. I started to have strange thoughts. It was weird to think that I had actually come out of that body. Biology is even stranger than physics sometimes. For example, people talk about how life began on the Earth by saying stuff like, "Well there was a one-celled creature and it evolved into all of us." But where did the one-celled creature come from? Did it evolve out of rocks?

Then my weird thoughts dried up, and my head emptied. I stood up and sat down, then I stood up and sat down again. I didn't know where to put myself. It was as if I was trying to get out of my body and go somewhere else, but of course I was unable to do so.

I became aware that I was grinding my teeth, something I normally do only in my sleep. My head was hot. I could feel the blood pumping in my ears. I looked at my hands. They were trembling slightly.

Looking back, I don't think I had ever felt so angry in my life. I was angry with stupid bloody adults who thought only of themselves. I was angry with stupid bloody Peaches for running out of the room, and I was angry with stupid bloody Melchior for not sitting down with me and talking to me like a grown-up.

Above all, I was angry at stupid bloody me for being so stupid that I couldn't do anything to stop them splitting up, and for not being able to work out why I had made it happen in the first place. Was I really so bad?

I got up again, and noticed the book and the words I had written down on the scrap of paper beside it. I stared at them. Suddenly it was obvious what they meant.

Everything is space, within and without.
The mirror is a wall that reflects all your doubt.
Run through that wall without any fear

For all that is solid will soon disappear.
Hold these words pressed hard to your heart.
The seen and unseen must surely part.

I understood now. The book wanted me to jump into the mirror.

It wanted me to hold the book and run through the mirror – without any fear.

That last part was easy. I was too angry to feel afraid. I thought that if I gave the mirror a good smashing, it might make me feel a lot better about myself, and it would also get rid of the stupid picture of me that it showed every time I looked into it – all small and scared and silly-looking, with black skin and nubby hair and a skinny, spotty body.

I grabbed the book and held it against my chest – hard to my heart. I was ten paces away from the mirror, and I didn't even think. I ran as fast as I could, head first, right into it, and waited for the sound of breaking glass to fill the air. That would show my mother there were more important things to do than take a stupid phone call when your son's head was about to explode.

But no sound of breaking glass came. Instead, there was silence, deep and dark.

CHAPTER FIVE

HOW TO BE INVISIBLE

Before I relate what happened next, I will continue explaining the Mystery of the Magic Atom Experiment. It will make it easier to believe what happened to me when you understand the improbable things that occur in nature.

I had reached the part of the explanation where the atom gun – or cannon, or Kalashnikov, or Thompson sub-machine gun – was firing atoms at a wall in front of which was a screen with two slits in it.

I know what I would *expect* to happen. If you fired a machine gun at a wall, in front of which was a bullet-proof screen with two slits in it, you would – obviously – expect to see *two* slit-shaped rows of bullet holes in the wall behind the screen instead of one.

That's exactly what you *would* get if you fired a normal gun at the wall and the slits were big enough to let bullets through.

But when you fire an atom gun at the screen with slits in, something completely different happens.

There are no lines of atom holes in the wall. There are no slit-shaped patterns.

What you see is a single swirly pattern of atom traces

spread all over the place, in fanning-out, overlapping, wave-like shapes.

It is as though you have not been firing atoms at the slit, but water bombs which have exploded on impact.

Imagine – the moment the atoms went through the slits, instead of going BAMABAMABAMA and slamming into the wall like bullets, they went SPLODGE SPLODGE SPLODGE, and suddenly turned into something like water which spread out like waves.

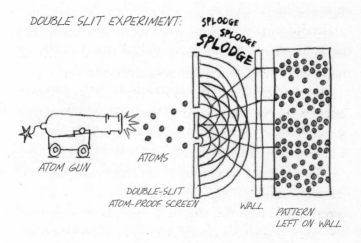

DOUBLE SLIT EXPERIMENT: SPLODGE SPLODGE SPLODGE

ATOM GUN

ATOMS

DOUBLE-SLIT ATOM-PROOF SCREEN

WALL

PATTERN LEFT ON WALL

Which is extremely weird. How can atoms fired through one slit behave like bullets and atoms fired through two slits behave like water bombs? Surely it has to be one or the other?

Or maybe not, you say. Maybe it's no big deal. After all, despite the fact that they are just small chunks of stuff, atoms are bizarre things. Maybe when the atoms go through two slits they bang into one another on the other side of the screen and explode or something, leaving a great splodgy mess on the wall instead of two nice neat little slit patterns – rather like bullets might smash into one another and explode into smithereens.

The scientists performing the experiment thought this might be the case too. Then they thought the atoms might be going SPLODGE SPLODGE SPLODGE because they were interfering with one another. So they repeated the experiment – but this time firing *only one atom at a time*.

They fired a single atom and waited until it had either bounced off the screen or gone through a slit and hit the wall. Then they fired another one, then another.

And so on, until – you might expect – they eventually got a double pattern of slit-shaped atom holes on the wall.

But that's not what happened.

When there was one slit there was a single long, slim pattern on the wall, as if little bullets had gone through the slit and hit the wall behind.

But when there were *two* slits, once again – SPLODGE SPLODGE SPLODGE. There were atom traces all over the place, making a pattern like waves on the wall.

The atoms weren't interfering with one another. They were *behaving differently* according to how many slits there were in the screen.

Which begged the earthshaking question: How did the atoms in the atom gun *know* that there was a second slit so that they could decide to behave like water bombs instead of bullets?

If you're a "so whatter" – one of those people who are

never prepared to be impressed by anything – then you'll say, "Who cares? It's just atoms, not real things. So what?"

But atoms are actually the reallest things there are. Are things less real because they are small? Obviously not, any more than things are more real because they are big.

No, atoms are real. Atoms are *you*. Atoms are as real and solid as the book – or the Kindle, or iPad – you are reading.

So how come they can "know" things – like how many slits there are in a screen – and behave differently according to circumstances?

This phenomenon is known in science as "particle/wave duality", which makes it sound perfectly reasonable until you realize that it is in fact totally bloody impossible and mad.

Anyway, just in case you're still not impressed, the Mystery of the Magic Atom does, in fact, get even weirder still. But I'll come back to that.

I guarantee, when I explain the next bit of the experiment, you will be utterly discombobulated.

"Discombobulated", incidentally, means "confused" or "disconcerted".

Back in my bedroom, I had become aware of a wobbling sensation, as if the tremors in my hands had spread to my whole body. I felt somehow that I had become one of those double-slit atoms – once solid, but now watery and spread out all over the place. For a moment, I had the sense that I was actually inside the mirror looking back into the room.

If I was inside the mirror, I had no idea how long I stayed there for. The sense of blankness came and went, and I was distantly aware of tiny scraps of stuff happening. I could feel the weight of the book still pressed against my chest. It felt dense and heavy, like a brick. I was vaguely aware of the noise of a far-off police siren. At one point, I saw a spectrum of colours, like light blazing from a prism, but it was only momentary, before everything went dark and silent again. I felt hot, then cold. There was a high-pitched whine in my head, like a giant asthmatic fly buzzing. I didn't feel afraid or surprised or even think it was weird. I just felt … nothing, really.

Finally, I felt myself falling. It seemed like I was falling a very long way, maybe hundreds of metres, through air that was clear and crisp – sort of mirror-air. But when at last I reached the ground, it wasn't the ground at all, it was my bedroom carpet. I was spread out on it like someone had dropped me from the ceiling, my arms and legs spreadeagled, one hand still holding on to the book, my face looking straight upwards.

I could hear footsteps thundering up the stairs, so I assumed I must have made a noise when I dropped out of the mirror. I couldn't move. I just lay there, on my back, staring at the ceiling. I felt very calm. I could still feel the book pressed against my heart.

The door burst open and Peaches stumbled in, looking panicked. She looked straight at me – then looked away again.

"What the hell was that noise?" she said out loud. I thought she must be talking to me, and I was about to answer when she spoke again.

She said, "Strato?" Then she opened the door and shouted out of it, "Strato, where are you?" Then she left again as quickly as she had arrived.

I lay there feeling completely peaceful. It was obvious to me, right at that moment and without any doubt, that I had somehow become invisible, and I accepted it as completely normal. It didn't feel odd. It was just that nobody could see me. It was one of those miracles that science couldn't explain, and I was positioned right at the heart of it.

I lay there a few minutes more, words and questions lazily drifting through my mind. There was a game, Poohsticks, that I used to play with Melchior at the canal bridge near our home in London. We would each drop a stick into the water on one side of the bridge and see which one emerged from the other side of the bridge first. My thoughts were like that – slow, lazy, barely moving.

So – I had become invisible. That was highly interesting. How long would I stay invisible for? How would I be able to become visible again? It was going to be a peculiar life if I wasn't able to return to my proper form. I might end up as a circus freak – the Amazing Vanishing Geek.

I eventually worked out that the answers were probably somewhere in the book that I was holding.

I raised my head and looked down at my own body. I appeared to be fully visible, which was surprising since, given Peaches' reaction, I wasn't. I cautiously stood up, feeling a bit dizzy, and looked in the mirror which I had presumably emerged from a few minutes earlier.

There was no reflection of me. I could see myself – but the mirror couldn't see me.

Again – interesting. I was determined to start making scientific observations about this curious thing that had happened immediately. It should not have happened – it was impossible in fact – but it *had* happened, and a good scientist has to accept data at face value. You can't prejudge – evidence is evidence.

If I was invisible, then how was it that my clothes were invisible too? Was it because I was touching them? But my skin wasn't touching all of them – I was wearing a sweater over my shirt. Also, that suggested that anything I touched would become invisible. I tried touching the wall, the table, the bed. Nothing happened – they were all still reflected in the mirror. It was clear that only what had gone into the mirror had been rendered invisible – me and my clothes and the book.

By now, I would have expected to become scared or panicky and scream for Peaches to come and help me. But I think my scientific training stepped in and kept things in perspective. Also, the transformation process itself seemed to have had some kind of calming effect.

Instead of panicking, I decided to ask myself a simple question: *What might I do, now that no one could see me?* Immediately, the obvious, if childish, answer came to me: I could become a superhero.

Stratoman.

The Amazing Invisible Boy.

The Vanisher.

They all had a nice ring. But I dismissed the idea immediately. I'm not really that way inclined. I'm a bit dull and domestic. I couldn't really imagine fighting crime, not even petty crime like shoplifting or littering or parking on double yellow lines.

What else could I do? It was shameful, no doubt, but the next thing I thought of was the chance I would have to sneak into the girls' changing rooms and see them without any clothes on.

Again, I tried to put that to one side. This experience was about science, not pleasure. I had to do some objective research on the world around me. The fun could be postponed till later.

I decided that as soon as Melchior came back to the house, I would show him what had happened to me and we would be able to investigate together – something I'd always wanted to do with my father.

I wasn't going to tell Peaches, though. She had a nervous disposition. She would probably drop dead of a heart attack there and then, or worse, call the police or an ambulance. She would certainly make a terrible fuss.

It then occurred to me that I was in a unique position. At a stroke I had outmanoeuvred the uncomfortable reality conjured by the double-slit.

Which reminds me. I haven't finished telling the story of the Mystery of the Magic Atom.

I had got up to the bit where the experiment revealed that if atoms went through one slit they behaved like bullets and if they went through two slits they behaved like water bombs, and no one could explain why. I told you it gets weirder still – and it does.

When the double-slit experiment was first performed, scientists were astonished to discover that atoms could a) be two things at once and b) somehow "know" whether there was a second slit in a screen or not. Being scientists, they took the shortest route to trying to find out how it happened.

They pointed a camera at the two slits as the atoms went through them, to see what occurred at the exact moment they changed from bullets to water bombs.

(It wasn't actually a camera. It was a different sort of recording device. But the principle is exactly the same, and so is the purpose – to observe what was going on.)

They pointed the camera at the two slits and waited for the bullet-like atoms to somehow turn into water bombs, as they had done in all the previous experiments.

But something amazing happened.

When they had a camera pointed at the slits – the atoms *didn't change*.

When anyone tried to directly observe the screen to see what was happening, the atoms, when there were two slits, behaved exactly like bullets – the way they did when there was only one slit.

DOUBLE SLIT EXPERIMENT WITH "CAMERA":

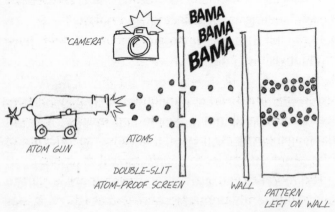

"CAMERA"

BAMA BAMA BAMA

ATOM GUN

ATOMS

DOUBLE-SLIT ATOM-PROOF SCREEN

WALL

PATTERN LEFT ON WALL

The splodginess had suddenly disappeared – because somebody or something was trying to take a look at what was going on.

When they took the camera away – water bombs. When they pointed the camera at the slits again – bullets.

The scientists could draw only one conclusion – *the atoms were somehow aware that they were being watched.*

(And also, presumably, the atoms didn't want to let on how they switched from bullets to water bombs).

This isn't science fiction. This is everyday, routine science.

The extraordinary conclusion one draws from this is that with atoms, the observer changes what is happening *just by the act of looking*. It becomes impossible to measure what is going on without affecting the result.

This was a result that not only astonished scientists, but scared them too, since it meant that the idea of the objective observer – which is what scientists like to believe they are – had to be abandoned.

"Objective", incidentally, means "not affected by personal feelings or prejudices; fair, unbiased".

Now tell me it's impossible that I could have turned invisible.

It struck me that I was in a uniquely privileged position. I could observe things – people and events – without changing them by my presence. Because the influence of being observed applies to people as well as atoms.

The moment you walk into a room, people start to behave differently simply because you are there. It is as if everyone has designed for themselves a series of different faces, and show different ones to different people, according to whether they are friends or enemies, strangers or family, powerful people or beggars.

Incidentally, the word "person" comes from the Latin word *persona*, which means "mask".

It is just like the Mystery of the Magic Atom Experiment. You can never know what people are really like because they transform themselves the moment you are interacting with them. You alter the reality simply by being there.

This is especially true of adults. I was just beginning to realize this – now that I was less of a child than I used to be. I was beginning to suspect very strongly that the faces adults showed to children were completely different from the way they actually were. That they were, in fact, acting, all the time, every day.

And the reason teenagers find it so hard being teenagers is that they have to negotiate that transition – from being real to being fake.

It was only a theory. But as I say, now I actually had a chance to test it, since I could observe people without influencing their behaviour. It was like having my own personal, portable two-way mirror.

I couldn't wait to tell Melchior. He was going to be so proud of me for this discovery.

CHAPTER SIX

USEFUL THINGS TO DO WHEN YOU'RE INVISIBLE

In common with most of the nerdy fraternity, I like lists. They make me feel in control and help me to get things organized. If there's one thing better than an experiment, it's a bloody good list.

So I decided to write down a list of possibilities.

I wrote a heading on a piece of paper:

Useful Things To Do Now I Am Invisible

I sat for a long time, with my pen poised over the paper (which would have looked very odd to anyone who walked into the room, since the pen wasn't invisible, so it was just floating in the air, from the outsider's point of view).

My pen might have been poised over the paper, but my head was as empty as deep space (although, come to think of it, deep space actually isn't empty at all – it's full of fields and forces and potentialities).

Then I finally worked out the first thing to put on the list, which was pretty straightforward.

1.   Tell Melchior.

I needed to get his advice and I was sure this was my chance to visit his new laboratory.

The next thing I wrote down on the piece of paper was:

2.   Find out how to become visible again.

This was clearly vital. I didn't want to end up a circus freak. It would be lonely being invisible. You would never get a girlfriend because girls wouldn't know if you were ugly or not. Your friends would be unable to quite trust that you weren't checking what they were saying behind your back.

Apart from that, you would simply be too odd for anyone to want to socialize with in the first place. It would make any friend, actual or potential, profoundly uncomfortable.

Imagine going to the cinema or a cafe with an invisible person. People would think you were mentally unstable for talking to the empty seat next to you, and would be terrified when a can of Coca-Cola rose up, hovered in mid-air and then emptied its contents into an invisible stomach.

No, remaining invisible on a permanent basis was clearly untenable. I decided that I had to work out how to get visible again and I hoped Melchior would be able to help me.

Coming up with a third useful thing to do was more difficult. I ran through the obvious ideas, some of them childishly trivial. I thought, for instance, that I could sneak into the cinema for free and watch 18-rated films. Again, the prospect of the girls' changing rooms presented itself to me, but the idea began to seem increasingly sordid. I may have been a geek but I wasn't a perv.

Then I thought I might go to Buckingham Palace and look at the Queen when she was just watching telly or having her breakfast. Or I could make my way into the *Doctor Who* studio, or the set of the new Johnny Depp movie, so I could really get to see celebrities close up.

The only trouble was, I wouldn't be able to tell anyone I was there, since they wouldn't be able to see me, and even if I did tell them – once I was visible again – they wouldn't believe me. They'd just call Security and get me thrown out. And anyway, I didn't know where the *Doctor Who* studio was, or where Johnny Depp was filming, or how to get to Buckingham Palace on my own.

So that was the silly part over with. I decided to take this matter more seriously. Somehow, I was sure I could use this to push forward the frontiers of scientific knowledge, although I couldn't work out how.

But all that could wait, I decided. Because at that point it occurred to me that the main thing I wanted to do was this:

3. *Find out why Lloyd Archibald Turnbull is picking on me and what I can do to stop it.*

I had come to the conclusion that the request to befriend me on Facebook was another ruse to humiliate me. I regretted accepting *all* the friend requests; I presumed the two Waynes – Fleet and Collingham – and Susan Julia Brown were friends of Lloyd Turnbull's, and I knew perfectly well in my heart of hearts that he was out to get me.

I sometimes fantasized about going on a body-building course, followed by a judo course, followed by a karate course, then confronting Lloyd Turnbull and giving him a good thrashing in front of all his friends – who would then all look at me in awe and terror – and then becoming the leader of all the toughest kids in the school so no one would ever pick on me again.

However, now I had no need to go on a body-building course, or learn martial arts. Because being invisible was better.

It meant I could find out about Lloyd Turnbull's weak spots – and that was something he was going to find very discomfiting. Once I knew his weak spots, I could employ psychological torture, which I was sure was the most effective kind to receive and very enjoyable to administer. I would be able to give him a dose of his own medicine.

For instance, perhaps he was secretly attracted to some girl and kept it deadly secret. Or perhaps he was a homosexual. (I had nothing against same-sex relationships, but if it would embarrass Lloyd Turnbull, then it was worth considering as a weapon.)

Or he might be secretly afraid of the dark. Or of spiders, or of starlings – like my mad uncle. I could gather all this kind of material easily and use it against him. It could be that Lloyd Turnbull had an embarrassing habit that nobody knew about – sucking his thumb when he was asleep, perhaps. Then if he started to pick on me, I could just start sucking my thumb and look at him meaningfully. That would certainly give him pause for thought.

I could go for a less subtle approach. Haunting would be an obvious option. If you were invisible, you had the perfect opportunity to impersonate a ghost. I would be able to make my way into his bedroom at night and, perhaps, start moving things about. Then I could let him know the next day at school that I knew about the moving things, and that would terrify him even more. I'd tell him that if he wanted it to stop, he'd have to stop bullying me – me and anyone else, because I was sure I was not the only one.

So that was Lloyd Archibald Turnbull taken care of.

Just then, another thing occurred to me. I needed to make sure that nobody – other than Melchior – found out that I could become invisible. Because that would be very bad, I realized. I'd seen *E.T.* enough times to know what happens when the scientific community makes some unsettling new discovery. I'd probably end up in a plastic bubble for the rest of my life, surrounded by men in white coats prodding at me. My parents wouldn't be able to stop them – the government is too powerful when it comes to that sort of thing.

I would have to guard my special power carefully. Melchior and I would be the sole keepers of the secret until we had worked out properly what to do with it, and understood its source and the properties of the book.

So this was the next goal:

4.	Don't let anyone know (apart from
	Melchior).

I did not feel these four goals were unrealistic.

For the first time in ages, I felt powerful, and in feeling powerful, I felt good.

Then a further goal occurred to me. It was extraordinary that I hadn't thought of it before, because it was the most important problem to solve of all, at least from a non-scientific, emotional perspective:

5.	Find out what has gone wrong between
	Melchior and Peaches and how I might
	fix it.

I was just about to elaborate on the point when I heard my mother downstairs, talking on the phone. I took a deep breath, exited my room and walked carefully down the stairs. She looked right at me, but she clearly still couldn't see me.

She seemed upset. It would have been unusual for me to leave the house without informing my parents. It would have been irresponsible. But she clearly thought the bad news she had given me had unhinged me in some way and that I had run away.

She would have been even more upset if she had actually known the truth, but all the same, I didn't like to see Peaches this distressed. She was actually crying.

I suddenly wasn't sure that I could wait for Melchior to come home before trying to work out how to become visible again. My mother was so worried about me – who knew what she might do? I turned round immediately and made my way back up to my room.

When I got there, I picked up the book. If it could tell me how to become invisible, surely it could tell me how to bring myself back into the visible world again. And it was weird, but I felt like the book was in some strange way interactive. It seemed to respond to what I wanted from it.

The book, as before, was blank when I looked at it directly. I stared at the cover where the tiny mirror was inset. It really was extraordinarily bright and sharp. But it didn't give me any clues as to how to make myself reappear. And as I could hear that my mother was getting more distressed by the moment, it was a matter of some urgency.

I was beginning to get slightly apprehensive that there might be no way back to visibility. So I held the book up to the mirror again – this time on the third page. And sure enough, once more, words appeared, looming and fading in the reflection as if they were made out of smoke. I had to look at them very carefully to see what it was they were saying, but after a while it was clear enough:

> To become the way you were before,
> Muster courage, let faith be sure.
> Hold the volume to your chest –
> The silver'd wall will do the rest.
> Throw thyself to the other side.
> Falter not, lest worlds collide.

Then the words disappeared as I'd thought they might the last time – but not before I had got them clear in my mind.

It seemed pretty straightforward. To stop being invisible I simply had to do what I had done before – hold the book against my heart and run full pelt into the mirror (that must be what was meant by "silver'd wall" – a mirror is glass backed with silver).

I turned the page to see if there were any other instructions. More words appeared, wavering and undulating as before.

> *A warning must be clearly took*
> *By those that wish to use this book.*
> *Do not be seen, or discovered, or let*
> *The secret be known lest thy power be forfeit.*

Then the writing disappeared. But the meaning was clear enough. The message was entirely unequivocal. If anyone found out about the book or what it could do, or discovered that I was capable of becoming invisible, then the power would be lost.

So much, then, for telling Melchior. The moment someone found out, I would lose the power – presumably for good.

This was a serious problem. But it was not my most immediate problem. I could still hear my mother weeping. Clearly something had to be done, and done right away.

I stared at the mirror apprehensively. Oddly, it wasn't so easy to run at it this time. I wasn't angry now – so angry that I didn't care what happened to me, so angry that I half wanted to smash the mirror to bits. This was different. To run cold-bloodedly into a sheet of glass – even if you've done it before – is not an easy thing to do. Furthermore, I couldn't be sure that it would work in reverse, whatever the book said.

After reasoning with myself for several minutes – which is to say, trying to get out of a state of panic – I realized that the more I thought about it, the more difficult I was going to find it to run into that mirror for a second time.

All at once, I emptied my mind, held the book up against my chest and ran full pelt into the sheet of glass on my wall.

There was no impact. The feeling was exactly the same as it had been the first time. The jelly feeling, the high-pitched whine, the sense, momentarily, of being inside looking out. The colours, the heat, the cold, the falling. Then I was back on the carpet again, flat on my face this time.

At that very moment, my mother walked into the room. As I looked up, her eyes widened and she ran to me and threw her arms around me, squeezing me so hard I thought my eyes were going to pop out.

"Strato! Where did you disappear to? Why are you lying on the floor like that? Are you sick? I thought you had run away. Don't ever do that again, you bad, wicked genius. I was so worried. Do you have any idea the effect it had on me?"

I mumbled something about going to post a letter, and she seemed to be satisfied with this, because after about five minutes she had recovered herself and was back tapping away at her computer, presumably working on her book. Peaches is not only very emotional, she is highly mercurial.

"Mercurial", incidentally, means "changeable" or "unpredictable".

My father turned up again thirty minutes later, carrying a bottle of wine, full of apologies. I heard him exchange a few words with Peaches, then rush up the stairs to my room. He burst in. The fact that I was in something of a state of shock did not appear to register with him.

"Strato, what on earth did your mother tell you?"

I told him that she'd said he was moving out. His lips went very thin.

"She had no right saying that to you. Nothing has been decided yet. Nothing at all. If something like that ever happened, I wouldn't just let Peaches tell you by herself."

I nodded. I let silence speak for me.

My father, in the meantime, seemed to be having difficulty finding the right words.

"Look, Strato, I won't pretend to you that things are easy. We're struggling. You know that. But we're doing our best. It's true that … well, me moving out for a while is one of the options that we've been looking at. But nothing is decided yet. We're working one or two things through. That's all."

He seemed to have more he wanted to say. But he had run out of words. So I decided to break the silence.

"But you might break up."

He looked thoughtful, as if contemplating a mathematical formula.

"Any couple might break up."

"But you're more likely to break up than most couples."

He sighed from somewhere very deep inside himself.

"It's possible, Strato. I won't deny it. But we're not quite at that point yet. OK, boy? OK?"

He tapped me on the end of my nose. Melchior doesn't like to hug me too much – he's not a very physical person. But I don't take it as any kind of gauge of his affection for me. Melchior is as solid and reliable as titanium.

I nodded and said I was OK. But I wasn't OK. I was lying.

Which meant that although I was only thirteen years old, I was already beginning to act like an adult.

After he left, I returned to my list. My train of thought had been interrupted. I racked my brains. I found myself running out of ideas.

You would imagine that once you knew how to become invisible there would be an endless list of things you could do, but it turned out actually not to be that simple. You are limited both by your imagination and your courage. As I have already said, I am not an imaginative person and I am not a particularly brave one either, which is probably why I seemed to attract bullies.

Thinking of bullies, one more thing suddenly occurred to me. The next and final thing I wrote on the piece of paper was:

6. Find out about Dr Nathan Walter Ojebande and why he is picking on me too.

CHAPTER SEVEN

DR NATHAN WALTER OJEBANDE

Dr Nathan Walter Ojebande was the only other black person in Hedgecombe. But he wasn't a child. He was a teacher.

He wasn't exactly a bully. He was just strict. I suspected that his intentions were good. But the effect on me was the same.

As it happened, he taught physics, my specialist subject.

Dr Nathan Walter Ojebande was well-spoken, with a slight rural accent and a soft, yet somehow penetrating voice. He had a cloud of white hair on his head. He was also religious, which struck me as odd for a science teacher, and he always carried a black leather-bound Bible with him into class. He prayed to himself silently at the beginning and the end of each lesson. Most of the teachers wore smart-casual clothes, but he always dressed in a black suit with a white shirt and a dark tie, like a funeral director. He almost never smiled.

For some reason, he had embarked on a vendetta against me from the moment I walked into his classroom. He always asked me the most difficult questions, and if I couldn't answer them properly then he got this look on his face like I was letting the side down, and he could be sarcastic to the point of rudeness. My supposition was that he thought that if he didn't pick on me, the other children would think he was giving me preferential treatment on account of us both belonging to the same ethnic group.

If you had set up a CCTV camera in the classroom, I don't suppose you would have been able to detect that Dr Ojebande was singling me out, but I knew, I just *knew*. Dr Ojebande wanted me to be the smartest child in the class, and when I wasn't, he got angry. But when I *was* the smartest child in the class, that seemed to make him angry too.

As I have already observed, adults really don't make a lot of sense, however much you study them.

What he didn't seem to realize was that although I probably was as bright as he believed me to be, it would not much contribute to my popularity if I was perceived by the other children to be showing off. So sometimes, even when I knew the answer to a question, I gave the wrong one.

Incidentally, Peaches had told me that it was Dr Ojebande who had told on me about playing truant. He had worked out that the sick notes I had forged were not in my parents' handwriting. Clearly, I had underestimated Dr Ojebande. I hadn't thought anyone would bother to check.

Given what I knew about Dr Ojebande, this truanting incident – which had amounted to no more than three days in all – seemed unlikely to improve our teacher/pupil relationship.

I assumed Dr Nathan Walter Ojebande felt that,

by truanting, I had been guilty of a form of betrayal. I guessed that – relying on my intuition rather than any concrete evidence – he thought I had conformed to some kind of negative ethnic stereotype that reflected badly on him as well as myself.

The day after I learned how to be invisible, I had a double period with Dr Ojebande, so I was bracing myself. Also, I had to get through lunchtime without Lloyd Archibald Turnbull finding me. It wasn't going to be easy, but it seemed that running away to browse in the town's bookshops during the day was no longer an option.

On the way to school, Mr Maurice Bailey, the bus driver, was behaving strangely as usual. He was cheerful and chatty, but his line of conversation was disconcerting.

"Morning, Stratters," he said, giving me a big grin and showing his tea-stained teeth as I put 50p in the slot.

I nodded, not sure what to say.

"Tell me something, Stratters," he said, holding up the bus until he'd finished talking to me. "Do you ever go sunbathing?"

This was a bloody weird question to ask, but I thought I might as well answer it just so he would start the bus and we could all get to school on time.

"Sometimes, yes."

"But why?" he said, still smiling. "What's the point?"

"It feels nice," I said.

"Do you use suntan lotion?" he said.

"Yes."

Mr Bailey seemed to be waiting for me to say something

else, so I scanned my brain for more details. I usually used my mother's – she never bought special cream for me.

"Ambre Solaire factor 12 coconut tanning oil," I said.

He looked puzzled and then he started laughing, as if the idea of me getting a suntan was the funniest thing in the world.

"Go on, Stratters, you nutcase. Sling your hook."

Then he put the bus into gear and drove on, still laughing like a lunatic.

The bus journey took the normal amount of time – seventeen minutes and twenty-four seconds, or thereabouts – and when we got to the school I exited the bus, keeping my eyes peeled for Lloyd Archibald Turnbull and his cohorts.

"Cohort", incidently, means "assistant" or "accomplice".

The school was a nice building – old, red brick – but it seemed quite large to me – there were maybe 600 pupils compared with the 200 at my school in London. I wasn't even interesting for my skin colour any more – for the first week or so people had stared at me, but now I suppose I was "part of the furniture".

Dr Ojebande's class came first. As usual, he was dressed in a black suit and dark tie. He quietly said his morning prayer to himself, gripping his Bible in his left hand, then he turned to the lesson. The subject was "the building blocks of matter". We were learning about how everything is made of particles and that there are forces operating between them, and that these particles move about more vigorously the hotter they get, and so on.

This was all pretty basic stuff to me. I was much

more interested in what the particles were made of, and what the particles that made up the particles were made of. That's where things get really weird, at the subatomic level.

Melchior often talks about this subject. He is not just any kind of common-or-garden scientist, but a particle physicist.

Or at least I believed he was at the time.

I could never fully comprehend what Melchior told me about science, but what I did understand was that things that look ordinary are actually anything but.

For instance, did you know that the universe is made almost entirely of nothing at all?

I like to ask big questions like "Why did the universe begin?" and "How are stars born?" because I think the big questions are the most interesting. One day, I had asked Melchior one of the biggest questions of all.

"Melchior," I'd said, "what is the universe made of?"

He'd said molecules, and I'd asked what they were made of, and he'd said atoms, and I'd asked what they were made of and he'd said electrons, protons and neutrons, and I'd asked what *they* were made of and he'd said subatomic particles like quarks and gluons, and I'd asked what they were made of, and he'd said: "Actually, pretty much nothing at all. Space mainly. Space and the electromagnetic force."

Then Melchior told me that if you took all the space out of a person what was left would be far smaller than a grain of salt. The fact that we don't all walk through walls and each other has more to do with the way forces repel or attract one another than the fact that objects are hard or solid.

He also said that if you sit on a chair, you are in actuality hovering a very small distance above it. Which seems hard to believe, but he swore it was the truth.

"Actually, at the very smallest level, right down where the subatomic particles are, things are constantly popping in and out of existence, which means that *you*," he said, tapping me on the nose, "since you're made of these particles, are constantly popping in and out of existence too. You're there. Then you're not there. And then you're there again. They call it 'Quantum Froth'. Like a sort of cosmic cappuccino." He laughed.

I said it sounded as if we were more like a dream, or a thought, than something solid.

He said, "That's a very grown-up thought. But then you do have very grown-up thoughts, don't you? It's easy to forget that you're only twelve years old."

Melchior must sound like a real know-it-all, but he isn't, actually. He often admits that scientists don't really know anything like as much as they say they do.

They don't know how life began, or what made the Big Bang happen, or how lumps of meat like you or me can do things like think and see and imagine and remember.

Science isn't really as boring as they make it sound in school – Bunsen burners and periodic tables and properties of compounds and stuff like that. When you come down to it, science is extremely interesting and not dull at all. At least, it is the way Melchior explains it.

Science is all about miracles, according to Melchior.

Of course, scientists don't believe in miracles. But my father does. He says that us simply being here is a miracle, that it would make far more sense if there was nothing at all forever. He thinks people like my mother make up miracles, like ley lines and spiritual auras, because they don't understand the magic that is all around them all the time.

What was on my mind that day in Dr Ojebande's physics class was the fact that eighty-three per cent of the known universe is made up of material we can't see or detect – dark matter and dark energy. This fascinated me, because apparently dark matter and dark energy are both there and not there, and that seemed to make no sense.

Dr Ojebande was a stickler for the curriculum and he didn't like going off-subject. All the same, after about five minutes of Dr Ojebande talking, I had a rush of blood to my head and, even though he hadn't asked the class a question, I put my hand up. I really don't know what came over me. I must have been very nervous to do such a bloody stupid thing. I think it was because Dr Ojebande always picked on me anyway. Perhaps I thought if I put my hand up it might pre-empt him asking me a difficult question which I would have to pretend not to know the answer to.

I don't think I've mentioned that Dr Ojebande is what is called "wall-eyed". This means that his eyes point in slightly different directions. One of his eyes seems bigger than the other, and he shifts this one – the left one – around the class like a radar. His gaze is very disconcerting – because of his multi-directional eyes, one gets the impression that he can see in two directions at once.

Another odd thing about his eyes is that they are green, like a cat's. And the eyeballs bulge out of their sockets somewhat. And when his gaze falls on you, it has the effect of rooting you to the spot.

When Lloyd Archibald Turnbull had been talking under his breath earlier in the lesson, all Dr Ojebande had had to do was fix his eye on him, and he shut up – although usually with other teachers he takes no notice.

After I put my hand up, that weird, green, roving left eye swung round in my direction. Two desks to my right, I could see Lloyd Turnbull and the two Waynes looking at me with slightly feral expressions on their faces.

"Feral", incidentally, means "wild" or "untamed".

Immediately to the right of me, Susan Brown was staring at me through her pink-rimmed spectacles and the curtain of hair that fell onto her face in a fashion that I had to admit I found bloody unsettling. Susan Brown was very pretty and innocent-looking – you would never have guessed that she could be one of Lloyd Turnbull's gang.

I glanced back at Lloyd Turnbull. I think he always enjoyed it when he saw Dr Ojebande about to pick on someone. Some people like going to comedy clubs to watch stand-up comedians. If there was a club for watching people being humiliated, I imagine Lloyd Turnbull would have paid to go to it.

There I sat with my hand held up in the air, already wishing that I'd kept it down, while those eyes made me feel about 50 centimetres tall (I am in fact 1 metre 44.5 centimetres). All the same, it was too late to back down, so I kept my arm raised until Dr Ojebande finally spoke.

"Mr Strato Nyman *esquire.* I don't think I've ever seen you put your hand up before. You must be feeling positively effervescent today."

There were a few stifled laughs from Lloyd Turnbull and the two Waynes. I mumbled something like, "Not really, Sir," and Dr Ojebande actually smiled quite kindly for once. Then I took a deep breath and began to speak. It was too late to stop now.

"Thing I was wondering, Sir, was … well, I was reading in one of my father's magazines that most of the universe is made up of stuff called dark matter and dark energy which you can't see and can't detect, and they know it's there because the universe is expanding so much faster than it should be, but my question is – if you can't see it or detect it, is it possible that dark matter isn't made up of particles at all, and then couldn't that mean that not everything that exists in the universe is made out of particles after all?"

There was what seemed like a very long silence, during which I conjured up a picture in my mind of me kicking myself – somehow – repeatedly on the rear end. How could I have been so bloody foolish as to draw attention to myself? It was better to stay invisible. The moment anyone noticed you, it gave them the chance to get you.

The words *Beam me up, Scotty* echoed through my head.

Eventually, after time seemed to stretch indefinitely, Dr Ojebande spoke.

"That's a very good question, Nyman."

I suppressed a smile. I looked over at Lloyd Turnbull, and he was grimacing.

"The answer, I suppose, is that it is perfectly possible that dark matter isn't made of particles, since no one has ever seen it or measured it. But the very fact that it is pushing the universe apart so quickly means that it certainly has mass. And every body with mass we have ever come across in nature is made of particles. Ergo, I think we can safely assume that dark matter – if anybody ever finds out what it actually is – probably is made of particles. Dark particles, I suppose."

He smiled – and that was it. No snide comments, no putdowns, nothing. He simply turned away and went back to teaching the lesson. I could hardly believe it. I had actually managed to please "Bandy", as the other children called him.

Maybe things were going to start getting better at the school after all.

However, that idea lasted exactly as long as it took to get out of the classroom, when I heard Wayne Fleet shout something I didn't understand at me across the corridor.

"Hey, DM. Nice to see that you've made friends with DE."

He turned away laughing, and I saw that his companions were laughing with him. It took me precisely eight seconds to work out what they were laughing at.

DM and DE. Dark Matter and Dark Energy.

Me and Dr Ojebande.

It's hard to keep feeling angry for very long, even if you're quite badly upset, as I was. It was such a stupid thing for them to say. But then the hurt wasn't in what they said, it was in the fact that they wanted to hurt me in the first place.

I decided to let it go. The way I saw it, everything is temporary. Even the biggest stars die. Feelings are more temporary than most things. You just have to wait for them to pass.

Also, I consoled myself by thinking that everything is in the past. Did you know, for instance, that when you look at the Sun, you're seeing it as it was about eight minutes ago, because that's how long it takes the light to get to the Earth? It seems such a strange thought. The Sun could have exploded five minutes ago, and you wouldn't know a thing about it. You would still be happily sunbathing, not knowing you had three minutes to go before you were vaporized.

And if you look through a telescope at a planet like Saturn, you are seeing it as it was about an hour ago.

This leads on to other strange thoughts. Just imagine – for the sake of this explanation – that there was a giant orchestra playing on Saturn. Of course, there couldn't be – it's too cold and the atmosphere is poisonous and there's no such thing as a giant orchestra. But if it was big enough to be seen through a telescope from Earth, you'd be able to see the musicians through the telescope performing a symphony, although actually on Saturn itself they might have finished the piece of music and gone back to the giant dressing room on the Sun to change clothes and go home.

Which is pretty strange. It means that everything you see – absolutely everything – is really in the past. By the time you see it, it has already taken place.

Which doesn't make a difference if you're only a few metres from someone, but when the distances are measured in light years, it has all sorts of weird implications.

(A light year is the distance light travels during one year. Light travels at 186,000 miles per second.)

For instance, it is a fact that many of the thousands of stars that you see when you look up in the sky have long ago burned out and disappeared altogether. All you're seeing is left-over light.

If you were far enough away from Earth and could look back through a big enough telescope, you could see the Tudors and the Stuarts and even the dinosaurs. Because light never dies – it just keeps flowing out through the vacuum of space forever.

These thoughts, weird though they were, consoled me. By the end of the day, I had stopped feeling angry. However, I was feeling sad instead.

I found myself wandering through the streets of the town again. When I'm a bit down, I like reading books that are too young for me, so I went into a bookshop that specializes in children's fiction and started reading one of the *Moomin* books by Tove Jansson. Even though they're a bit babyish, I've always enjoyed the Moomins because they are so completely bizarre.

On this occasion, I was reading about this creature called the Groke, who was very lonely and made everything around her go cold when she came near. The Groke was a weird-looking thing with cold, staring eyes. She was shaped a bit like a platypus, only somewhat furry. She had a long row of teeth and a triangular nose, and she looked frightened all the time. She had a tail, but none of the Moomins had ever seen her tail. No one ever went near her. She moved very slowly but never stopped moving. Wherever she stood, the ground froze and plants died. All the Groke ever wanted was friendship and warmth, but everyone shunned her, and she spent most of her time in her cave on top of the Lonely Mountains.

Poor old Groke. Who could bear to live a life like that? All the same, I couldn't help but wonder if it was really her own fault that nobody bloody liked her.

When I got home, I decided to try out my new power.

But before I did, out of habit, I checked my computer. And my sadness increased exponentially.

"Exponentially", incidentally, means "growing rapidly".

Lloyd Archibald Turnbull had posted a picture from a science book on his news feed. It was an illustration of the universe, highlighting "dark matter". It showed a network of stars spread like veins in a body with dark patches in between. This was meant to be an artistic representation of what dark matter would look like if you could see it, which you can't.

The caption, highlighted by Turnbull, included the words, "some scientists question whether dark matter even exists". And he had added "Dark Matter Nyman".

Obviously he was talking about me.

I trailed my cursor over to the unfriend button and clicked it, and then I did the same for the two Waynes. I was about to do the same for Susan Brown when

I noticed that I had a message. I opened my inbox and saw that the message was from Susan Brown.

All it said was, "Lloyd Turnbull is a brain-dead numpty. Don't take any notice of him."

I was suspicious. Lloyd Turnbull had initially used indications of friendship in order to get under my skin, and it was quite possible that Susan Brown was doing exactly the same thing, perhaps under the aegis of Turnbull himself.

I decided to give her the benefit of the doubt for the moment and returned to thoughts of being invisible. I decided to find out what was tearing our family apart and if it was all my fault.

Since it was a Thursday, I was fairly sure that Peaches and Melchior would be staying home. Melchior played bridge on a Monday, sometimes they went to the cinema together on Tuesday, Peaches did yoga on a Wednesday and pilates on a Friday and anything at all could happen at the weekend. But nothing ever happened on a Thursday night. So they would be downstairs together, and as it was only a day after they had apparently come within a whisker of ending their marriage, I was sure they would discuss whatever it was that was causing problems between them.

I like to keep a fairly conservative bedtime schedule. I go to bed at around nine o'clock. I decided that after supper I would brush my teeth, put on my pyjamas, stick my head in the front room to say goodnight and then pretend to read to myself for a while as usual before turning out the light.

*

What I was actually going to do was throw myself headlong into the bedroom mirror.

And then my experiment could begin, so that I could start to accumulate some empirical evidence to test the validity of the following three hypotheses:

1. Peaches and Melchior were going through a difficult patch but were not about to separate.
2. Peaches and Melchior were, in fact, about to separate.
3. It was all my fault.

"Empirical", incidentally, means "based on observation and experiment". This is the opposite of making elaborate, clever guesses.

Empiricism means you have to build up a body of solid, verifiable evidence before you can start making predictions. If that involved me invading Peaches' and Melchior's privacy, that was simply a sacrifice they were going to have to make in the interest of scientific inquiry.

After all, they had invaded my privacy often enough – barging into my room without asking, checking my computer to make sure I hadn't been accessing sexy websites, going through my pockets to see if there were any more forged sick notes. Now it was their turn, and I was going to employ the same defence they always used: it was for their own good.

CHAPTER EIGHT

THE PARENT TRAP

At approximately 9.02 p.m., I rose from my bed, picked up *How To Be Invisible*, held it hard against the jacket pocket of my pyjamas and hurled myself at the mirror. A few minutes later, I was heading down the stairs into the hall.

Luckily, the door to the front room was open, so I didn't have to wait until someone went in or came out. A door opening by itself would obviously have been extremely suspicious, and I needed no reminding that if I was found out, my power would immediately disappear.

Peaches and Melchior were just sitting there in front of the telly, with their dinner on little round wooden tables in front of them. The dinner hadn't actually been cooked – it was one that you bought from a supermarket and heated up in the oven. It was Melchior's night to cook and Peaches had made the sensible decision of insisting on something edible.

I was being as quiet as I could, and the television – a documentary about insects in the rainforest – was on quite loud, so I wasn't too worried about being heard. But I needed to find a spot in the room where no one would have reason to collide with me.

There was a "dead" corner in the room, in a recess on one side of the fireplace, which no one ever had any reason to go into. There were no domestic appliances there, or even electrical plug sockets, neither were there any bookshelves. I walked very quietly over to that corner, hoping that the floorboards wouldn't creak.

Although I couldn't see the television directly, I could see its reflection in the mirror over the sofa that Peaches and Melchior were sitting on. On the screen, a beautiful, delicate, leopard-spotted butterfly was making its way between purple trumpet-shaped flowers. It was a very happy and idyllic scene.

Then a bird the size of a small cat and the colour of a rain cloud swallowed it whole.

I tried to put the image out of my mind and concentrate on Melchior and Peaches. Although I was directly in the eye-line of both, neither of them appeared to notice anything unusual, even though it sounded to me like my breath and my heartbeat were both making a deafening noise.

I stood in the corner of the front room for more than an hour, waiting for a conversation to start. But nothing happened. Not once did they speak. It was bloody boring. I tried to keep myself amused by watching the television in the mirror. On-screen, the carnage continued – big insects eating little insects, frogs eating big insects, giant spiders eating frogs. Nature was beautiful, but it was a slaughterhouse. Small things didn't stand a chance.

The silence settled like snow. I was painfully aware of

an "atmosphere" – a generalized, unspoken bad feeling in the room.

There were only three occasions when they spoke during that time. The first was when Melchior asked Peaches to pass him the salt. She simply ignored him. Perhaps she wanted him to cut down, since salt can be bad for your blood pressure. However, Melchior's reaction – a grimace of irritation and a theatrical reaching for the salt cellar across the table – suggested to me that he knew Peaches did not have his health primarily at heart in ignoring his request.

The second time they spoke came shortly after an unfortunate incident that almost broke my cover. I'd made myself Heinz baked beans for supper that night – like I say, it was Melchior's night to cook – and I was experiencing problems with my digestion. At about 9.33 p.m. I broke wind. The emanation was perfectly soundless, but there was no mistaking the pungency of the odour that was slowly infusing the room, like one of the vaporous mists that filled the streets in the autumn.

After nearly a minute had passed, Peaches asked Melchior if he had "cut the cheese". This was an American expression my mother used. Melchior denied it. Peaches became heated, saying, "You can't even tell the truth about something as simple as that." Melchior continued to insist that he was innocent. Then they fell back into an angry silence again.

Shortly after that, Peaches asked Melchior what time it was and Melchior informed her that there was a clock in the kitchen if she wanted to know, and that appeared to be the end of the conversation for the night.

Once Melchior and Peaches had finished their food, they didn't even bother to clear up the plates, like they always told me I had to. They just left them there and slouched back on the sofa, one at each end with a gap of a metre between the two of them.

I was getting tired by then. The television had been turned off and concentrating on keeping still and quiet was becoming very tedious. I felt myself yawning repeatedly and had decided to give up and go to bed. But just as I was about to leave, my parents produced a little scrap of a conversation that was quite instructive.

Melchior got up as if to leave the room, but then he turned and said, "I know it's difficult, Marie-France. But it would be good to at least try to talk, don't you think?"

Peaches didn't say anything at first. Then after several more seconds had passed, she said, "We'll only fight."

"That's up to us, isn't it?" said Melchior.

"What do you want to talk about?" Peaches asked.

"Everything, I suppose," he replied.

"I'm very tired," said Peaches.

"You're always tired when we need to talk," said Melchior.

Peaches sat up straight with a not-very-nice gleam in her eye, and said, "Well go ahead then, Mel. What's eating you? Spit it out. Spill the beans. Solve the equation."

Melchior sighed in just that same deep, bone-tired way he'd sighed when he had talked to me in the bedroom.

"It doesn't matter."

Peaches, who only a few seconds previously had

been supposedly too tired to talk, said, "Come on then, let's hear it."

Melchior said, "What are we going to do about Strato?"

My stomach lurched.

"What do you mean, 'What are we going to do about Strato?'" Peaches said.

"If the worst comes to the worst. He's obviously upset and worried. Yesterday he hid and you couldn't find him."

"He just went out to post a letter."

"That means he left the house without telling anyone, which is out of character. And then there's the truanting. He never truanted from the school in London."

"What are you saying? That you want to move back to London?"

"No, I'm not saying that."

Then Peaches' angry expression slipped for a moment, and she looked momentarily sad. "Will the worst come to the worst? Perhaps we're both just having a difficult time adjusting."

"Adjusting to what?"

"Don't be obtuse, dahlin'. To moving down here. To you changing your job. To living with our past."

"Everyone has a past to live with."

"Not everyone has a past like ours."

"What's different about ours?"

"It's different because it was so recently the present."

By then I had lost the thread of the conversation entirely.

Then Melchior said, "We *do* need to consider the worst case scenario."

Then Peaches looked angry again and said, "You should have considered that before there *was* a worst-case scenario."

Melchior fiddled with the nose clamps on his glasses, a habit he has when he's feeling at a loss.

"Let's talk about it tomorrow. I'm too tired to jump over all the hurdles you're putting up right now. But promise me that we *will* talk about it. Because we can't keep pretending that—"

He didn't finish his sentence, because Peaches interrupted him.

"Stop being so melodramatic, Melchior," she said.

Melchior ignored this. "I need you to promise, Marie-France."

Peaches yawned. "What *you* need is a kick in your fat, lecherous ass."

Melchior just stared at her. Eventually she gave just the hint of a nod.

"Fine. OK. Good. Whatever you say."

"When?" said Melchior.

"Everything's got to be logged and catalogued with you, hasn't it? Nice and precise with clean edges. Shall we say 7.03? Or 7.08? Or 8.12? Is that good for you? 8.12?"

"Just tell me *roughly* when."

Peaches yawned and stretched.

"You're always nagging me. You want everything nailed down. Life isn't like that. There's nothing to nail it to. It happens in its own way."

"Please, Peaches. Make a commitment. For Strato's sake."

Peaches sagged back into the sofa.

"After dinner tomorrow, when I get back from pilates."

Melchior paused for a moment, then left the room and went up to bed without another word.

Peaches turned on the television again. The news was on and she just sat there staring at it. She paused the image on a picture of a man with an angry face who was demonstrating against something or other.

After several minutes, she took the image off pause, and switched to some old movie. It must have been a sad one, because she started weeping. I didn't want to watch the film, so I decided to go to bed.

Then I realized that I was unable to go to bed. Because Melchior had closed the door behind him, and there was no way for me to get out without making it look like there was a ghost in the room.

I was so enervated, I thought I was going to keel over there and then, but after about fifteen minutes Peaches yawned, dried her eyes with the back of her hand, switched off the television, opened the door and headed for the kitchen.

"Enervated", incidentally, means "weakened" or "exhausted".

She closed the door behind her, but once I heard that she was in the kitchen, I took the chance and opened it again, closed it behind me, and bolted back up to my room. There I grabbed the book, held it to my chest and ran into the mirror. Immediately, I was back to being visible.

It hadn't been a completely wasted evening, I decided, as I crawled as quietly as I could back under the covers, hiding the book beneath my pillow. I'd learned something important about being invisible – make sure you're not stuck in a room with a closed door, because you might not be able to get out again.

Also I had learned what the word "lecherous" meant. Since I hadn't heard it before, I looked it up. It means "lewd, lustful, lascivious or libidinous".

I had no idea why Peaches thought Melchior's fat ass was lecherous though. Anyway, his ass wasn't fat. It was so thin he hardly had an ass.

But I hoped to find out pretty soon. Peaches had promised to talk with Melchior about the Big Problem Between Them the next night, so I would find out all about it then. It gave me butterflies in my stomach to think that I would finally get to discover the big secret.

But as it turned out, I was very late getting home the next day. Because another opportunity came up – one that was just too good to be missed.

CHAPTER NINE

MY BOWELS EXPLODE

I often talk to myself. Inside my head, not out loud. Everybody does, presumably.

I might say to myself in a stern, reproachful voice, "You really must try harder to be less shy." Or when I get angry about something, I say to myself in a soothing voice, "Just take it easy."

It's commonplace. But who is talking to whom?

If there are two voices inside your head, are they both real, or is only one real? Or are they actually both the same voice?

If they are the same, why does one ask questions and the other answer them? Why does one voice ask for reassurance and the other offer it? Why does one urge and cajole and nag and the other try to do what it is told?

How can a voice exist in the first place when there are no vocal chords to create it, only brain cells, and no ear to listen to it, only more brain cells?

This confuses me. I've read too many science books that tell me there's no such thing as "me" in the first place, let alone two "me"s, because you can't empirically study the mind – it is not physical. The mind has no substance of any kind. Therefore it cannot logically exist. And yet it must do, because I am thinking all the time.

Only the brain exists, because it is material, and something that is not material cannot by definition exist. Yet even with modern CAT scanners that monitor the brain's activity, only a very small amount can be known about such a very complex organ. We know virtually nothing about how it generates consciousness.

The morning after I had eavesdropped on my parents, I said to myself, "You had better be careful with this invisibility experiment – perhaps there is stuff it is better for you not to know." Which I considered was a mature thought to be imparting to my other self who, unfortunately, wasn't really listening. But the dialogue stopped sharply as soon as I checked my Facebook page.

On my home page, there were three words in capital letters: I AM GAY.

I blushed. Doubtless Mr Maurice Bailey would have thought it amusing that I could blush, since he thought it peculiar that I might get a suntan.

I knew perfectly well that it was possible to hack into people's Facebook accounts and leave misleading messages, but I had never been a victim. I removed the post immediately and hoped that no one had seen it. It was almost certainly Lloyd Archibald Turnbull doing this, or one of his gang – one of the two Waynes or possibly Susan Brown.

I was unsure what to do. I could not report this to the

school authorities – it would be too embarrassing, and I had no proof that it was Lloyd Turnbull or his cohorts anyway. Furthermore, I was aware that snitching, or "grassing up" as it is known among the criminal fraternity, is taboo among schoolchildren.

I was also morally confused. Is it really an insult to say someone is gay? In my case it was simply inaccurate. I suspected it was intended as an insult though, and that was enough to make it upsetting.

But I had no time to think about it, because I had to hurry off to school. The bus was due in a few minutes. I grabbed my copy of *How To Be Invisible* – who knew when it might come in handy? – and stuffed it into the bottom of my book bag.

Within seconds of my reaching the stop, the bus arrived with Mr Maurice Bailey driving. I entered through the automatic doors, and he smiled as usual. Then out of the blue he said, "What kind of car does your dad have?"

"Pardon?" I said.

"Is it a BMW?"

I didn't know why he would have thought that.

"No," I said. "It's a five-year-old Mitsubishi, silver-grey, with a 1597cc engine."

He snorted.

"Foreign rubbish. Well, they're all foreign now. One part comes from China, another from India. Do you know what I drive when I'm not driving this bus?"

I said I had heard that he drove a jeep.

He looked disgusted.

"Who told you that? A jeep? Yankee scrap metal. No.

My baby is a 1952 Series 1 Land Rover, British made. A real classic. None of your foreign junk."

I nodded as if I knew what he was talking about and hurried off to go and sit down.

The bus was very full that morning. In fact there was only one seat free.

That seat was next to Susan Brown, who was staring at me fixedly from behind the lenses of her pink-rimmed spectacles.

I decided I would stand, but Susan Brown shifted over towards the window, clearly implying that I should join her. I felt conflicted. For one thing, I was fairly convinced – despite her sympathetic message – that Susan Brown was "in" with the Lloyd Turnbull coterie.

"Coterie", incidentally, is another name for "gang".

But more disturbing than the suspicion that Susan Brown wasn't to be trusted was the growing recognition that I was physically attracted to her. She was extremely pretty – at least to my way of seeing. She had big eyes peeping out from behind her glasses and clear skin, apart from a peppering of freckles on her nose, and a sort of smile that I thought was very calm and reassuring.

So I had one of those conversations with myself. It went like this.

Me 1: Why don't you sit with her?

Me 2: Because she's friends with Lloyd Archibald Turnbull and I can't trust her.

Me 1: It's only a bus journey. You don't have to trust her.

Me 2: There's no room on the seat.

Me 1: That's not true.

Me 2: I'm happy standing up.

Me 1: No, you're not.

Me 2: I'm too shy to sit next to her.

Me 1: Don't be a baby.

Me 2: I think I'll just stay here.

Me 1: Sit down, you baby.

Me 2: Who are you calling a baby?

Me 1: You.

Me 2: I'm not taking that from you.

Me 1: Do something to prove me wrong, then.

Me 2: I might.

Me 1: Go on then.

Me 2: I don't have to do what you tell me.

Me 1: Baby.

That was simply rude. I wasn't going to take that from me. So I sat down next to Susan Brown, making sure that there was a suitable distance between me and her – so much so, that half of my bottom was hanging off the edge of the seat.

For the second time that day, I was blushing deeply. At the same time, I felt happy to be sitting next to her, even if, as was quite probable, she was in league with my nemesis, Lloyd Archibald Turnbull.

A "nemesis", incidentally, is "an unbeatable opponent or a source of harm".

We sat there in silence for two stops, during which time I simply stared at the floor. My rational mind seemed not to be functioning very well. Then, as we approached the third stop, she spoke to me.

"Where do you live then, Strato Nyman?"

Her voice was, quite objectively speaking, lovely, like

words set to a tune. It was a soft voice, but surprisingly clear – I could hear it over the roar of the bus engine. And it held something in it that made me somehow slightly bolder. I looked up at her. She was smiling pleasantly.

"One hundred and seventeen Devonshire Crescent HP3 7FS."

It felt like the stupidest thing I had ever said in my life. But Susan Brown didn't giggle or laugh at me. She simply replied, "That's only a few streets from me. I must get on the stop before your one."

"Yes," I said, racking my brains for something more interesting to say. But nothing would come. We fell back into silence for a while.

Then, just as we were reaching the fifth stop, Susan Brown said to me, "Is Lloyd Turnbull still giving you a hard time?"

I shrugged as if I hadn't noticed whether he was or not.

"I saw that mean trick he pulled on Facebook. I know what he was getting at. 'Dark Matter.' He seemed to think it was hilarious."

I said nothing.

"Actually, I feel a bit sorry for him because of his bad arm. He wasn't like this before the car accident. I think it makes him feel he has to go on the attack before anyone attacks him first. Also, his mother is a gorgon."

A gorgon, I knew, was a mythological female creature with hair made of venomous snakes and a face so hideous it turned anyone who saw it to stone.

"I don't really mind about him," I heard myself say.

Again, my two selves were having a fight, one of them kicking the other brutally on the shin. Because if I did really mind – and I *did* – why wasn't I saying so?

Suddenly I had a moment of insight into why grown-ups lie so much – because they don't know why they're doing it, or even *that* they're doing it.

"You should have minded," said Susan Brown.

Now my two selves were having another argument. One self was saying to the other, "Should I tell her about the new post this morning?" And the other one was saying, "No, definitely not." And the first one was saying, "Don't be such a coward." And the second one didn't have a chance to reply because then Susan Brown said something else.

"Have they done anything else on Facebook?"

Now my radar was on. Was she simply acting as an agent for Lloyd Archibald Turnbull and the two Waynes? Did they simply want to check that hacking into my account had had the intended effect – to make me upset? My two selves went at it again.

Me 1: Tell her.

Me 2: No – she's not to be trusted.

Me 1: But you have to trust someone.

Me 2: Why? Why do I have to trust someone?

"Yes," I said, cutting my thoughts off in mid-train. "They hacked into my account this morning and updated my status to say that I was gay."

At that very moment the bus shuddered to a halt, and there was a clamorous huddle of people getting off. Susan Brown dropped her bag. I checked my watch. I was late, and I had Dr Ojebande first. If I was late for him, he would punish me for it all through the lesson.

I could not hang around waiting for Susan Brown to

find her bag. I joined the throng and headed for the door. I hoped upon hope that Susan Brown was on my side instead of Lloyd Turnbull's. But it isn't easy to trust someone. Every time you do and they let you down, it gets harder to trust someone else the next time, until one day you don't trust anybody at all.

As soon as I left the bus, I felt the most overwhelming desire to evacuate my bowels. I didn't know if it was out of nervousness, or whether there had been something wrong with the mushroom omelette Melchior had made me for breakfast. Peaches had insisted on picking her own mushrooms since we'd moved down here, but I wasn't sure she knew the difference between a chanterelle and the death cap, the former being delicious and the latter being fatal. Either way, there was nothing for it. Even though it would make me even later, I had to stop off at the boys' room, where my bowels virtually exploded for thirty seconds non-stop.

Five minutes later, I made it into the class. Everybody was seated and the lesson had begun. Dr Ojebande turned his bulging green eyes on me. He ran his hand exasperatedly through his ice-white hair. He tapped his black Bible impatiently with his finger in a very ominous fashion. But I barely noticed. I could not take my eyes off Susan Brown.

She had taken a seat directly next to Lloyd Archibald Turnbull.

Now I was certain that Susan Brown and Lloyd Turnbull were in cahoots. I couldn't help but stare. Lloyd Turnbull gave me a small, mocking grin. Susan Brown looked impassive. I tore my gaze away, and made my way towards an empty seat, eyes glued to the floor.

"Nice of you to join us, Mr Nyman," said Dr Ojebande softly, now looking pointedly at his watch. It was an old-fashioned pocket watch that he kept in a small pocket of his suit, apparently designed just for that purpose.

I mumbled a barely audible apology and sat down.

"Is there any particular reason you would like to share with us as to why, when every other student in the class made it to their desk on time, you, with all your alleged intellectual gifts, could not do the same?"

He replaced the watch in its special pocket and stared at me accusingly.

I said nothing. I was feeling too sick and too shy. I could hardly say that I had been stuck in the toilet.

"Well?" Dr Ojebande's voice took on a harder tone.

"No, Dr Ojebande," I mumbled.

"Pardon?" said Dr Ojebande. He waited.

I said nothing.

"I thought since you are 'gifted and talented' that you would be able to articulate yourself better. That is right, isn't it, Mr Nyman? You are gifted and talented? Is that not the case?"

I mumbled something again, not knowing what to say.

"He said, 'Mumble mumble glup bibble,'" said Lloyd Turnbull.

The rest of the class laughed, although I noticed that Susan Brown did not.

Now Dr Ojebande turned his swivelling eye on Lloyd Archibald Turnbull.

"I have already had to re-seat you this morning for

your insolent behaviour, Mr Turnbull. It appears to have had no inhibiting effect on you. Therefore, I would like you to join Mr Nyman in a one-hour detention this evening."

"Arse!" said Lloyd Archibald Turnbull, pretending that he was sneezing.

"I beg your pardon?" snapped back Dr Ojebande, his whole body tensing, leaning forward now towards Lloyd Turnbull. His hands closed around the Bible as if he was going to fling it at him.

"Yes, sir," said Lloyd Turnbull sullenly.

With that, Dr Ojebande's hand slowly released his Bible. His grey, heavy eyelids flickered, and then he turned back to the blackboard and began to write.

The rest of the day passed uneventfully. Encouragingly, nobody made any remarks about my Facebook status. Perhaps I had removed it quickly enough, although presumably whoever had posted it would be able to do it again if they so chose.

I rang Peaches on my mobile phone to inform her that I was going to be late on account of the fact that I had been given a detention. She seemed unconcerned. I believe I had disturbed her while she was working on her book, and when she is writing she really takes very little interest in anything or anyone else.

School finished at 3.30 p.m., and I walked towards the detention room, clutching my book bag to my chest – I was nervous of anything happening to *How To Be Invisible*. When I reached the room, Dr Ojebande hadn't arrived yet, but Lloyd Archibald Turnbull was sitting at one of the desks, picking at a spot on the back of his bad hand. He looked up briefly when I entered, then went back to picking at the spot. I found a desk four rows away, slightly to the rear of him, and sat down, still holding my bag.

After a few minutes, Dr Ojebande still hadn't arrived. At that point, to my surprise, Lloyd Archibald Turnbull turned his head and spoke.

"Do you want a stick of gum?"

I looked up and he was holding out a packet of Wrigley's chewing gum.

I decided not to mumble this time. I think my confession to Susan Brown had loosened me up a bit.

"You just want to get me into trouble."

Lloyd Turnbull shrugged. All the same, I reached out and took the gum, although I decided not to open it. I put it in my pocket. Lloyd Turnbull smiled, unwrapped another stick of gum and put it in his mouth.

Emboldened by the fact that he had spoken to me politely in the first place, I decided to risk a question.

"Turnbull?"

He turned lazily to look towards me, his jaw working on the gum

"Nyman?"

"What have you got against me?"

I could hear my voice quaver slightly as I asked this. My blink rate became frenetic.

He smiled in a perfectly friendly fashion, chewing slowly, then turned again towards the front of the room and spoke without looking at me.

"I don't know what you're talking about."

At that moment, Dr Ojebande walked into the room, and without missing a beat or even apparently looking in our direction, he said, "Turnbull, take that gum out of your mouth and dispose of it immediately."

Lloyd Archibald Turnbull did as he was told, rising from his chair with a studied slowness and putting the gum into a litter bin at the front of the room. Then he went and sat down again while Dr Ojebande stood there, sorting out some papers.

Dr Ojebande fixed one of his eyes on each of us, which must have been difficult to do since we were sitting a good three metres apart. But then that is one of the advantages of being wall-eyed, I dare say.

"I don't know what's going on between the two of you, but I want it to stop, right now."

Lloyd Turnbull looked innocent. I, predictably, looked at the floor.

Dr Ojebande turned to Lloyd Turnbull.

"Turnbull. You're not a bad boy despite what you obviously think of yourself. You are clever and articulate. I know that life hasn't been easy for you since your accident. And I know that your home life isn't always perfect."

It was Turnbull's turn to blush. He shifted on his chair slightly as if very uncomfortable.

"The solution to your problems is not taking out your frustration on other children. In the long run, it will simply make you unpopular, although in the short term it may attract some of the stupider children into your circle. Children who are not worthy of you."

Lloyd Turnbull just sat there, now looking resentful, as if Dr Ojebande had spoken out of turn. I was certainly surprised that he had revealed such intimate details of Turnbull's life in front of me.

Now he turned his attention to me.

"Nyman."

He paused as if uncertain what to say. He pursed his lips.

Finally, he said in a quiet, serious voice, "Nyman. Some people are natural victims. Not because they are members of an ethnic minority, or because they are under, or indeed over, endowed with certain gifts such as intelligence or physical grace. Some people are natural victims because they indulge in self-pity, and compensate for their lack of popularity by imagining that they are superior to others. You are not superior to others and you are not inferior. You are just a boy, like any other. Behave like one, and you will find that you will be respected, and, in the long run, liked – or if not liked, then at least accepted by your peers."

He paused as if trying to decide what to say next. He coughed, then spoke again, even more softly this time.

"I understand perfectly well that you are shy. Perhaps you have good reason to be. But shyness is a choice, not a medical condition. I can't teach you how to be more assertive. I can only tell you that keeping your head down and trying to avoid everyone's attention will only have the opposite effect in the long run."

This seemed to complete Dr Ojebande's speech. I waited for him to give us some lines to copy or something else to do. But instead he sat down behind the desk.

"I don't want to let you both off the hook by giving you

any work to do. I just want you to sit there for an hour, quietly. Spend your time reflecting on what I have said."

Dr Ojebande looked up at the clock on the wall.

"The hour begins now."

Turnbull looked agitated. "But Dr Ojebande, you were five minutes late and we were on time, so it isn't fair that you…"

"You will stay an extra five minutes, Turnbull. Don't speak again or I'll add another ten minutes."

Dr Ojebande knew how to punish. Any kind of tedious homework would have been better than just sitting upright at our desks, staring in front of us and doing nothing. My mother is an evangelist for the practice of meditation, which is basically the same thing. But I cannot see the appeal myself. The hour passed with extraordinary slowness. I had lots of internal conversations between me and myself, but they were entirely without interest. Then, at 4.41 p.m., Dr Ojebande looked up from his black Bible and dismissed me.

I rose and made my way towards the door. Lloyd Turnbull threw me a glance as I left. Oddly, it didn't seem hostile. It was more like a conspiratorial "I hate him – don't you?" I kept my face impassive and left the room.

Once again, my stomach seemed to be upset. I spent several minutes in the bathroom feeling unwell. After I had washed my hands, I emerged into the corridor again. Through the window I could see Lloyd Turnbull's mother behind the wheel of an old, dust-coloured Ford Focus parked outside the school gates. She was clearly waiting to pick Lloyd up.

It was then that I had the idea. This was an opportunity I didn't want to miss.

I made my way back into the bathroom, where there was a full-length mirror, and took *How To Be Invisible* out of my bag. I braced myself, faced the mirror and got ready to run.

Then a thought struck me. I knew the book worked in my bedroom, but what if it didn't work in here?

There was no time to think about it. I held the book to my chest and ran at the mirror.

Seconds later, I found myself sprawled on the floor of the bathroom. I stood up and looked in the mirror. Nothing. The magic had worked again. Without another pause, I headed out of the door. I could see Lloyd Turnbull getting into the front seat of the car beside his mother. She had her mouth open, apparently shouting at him.

I ran out of the school gates. Lloyd Turnbull's mother was still yelling at him. He looked very different to how he looked in school. Instead of being cocky and self-assured, he looked afraid. She was skinny, with muscled arms. Her head seemed slightly too big for her body, and her hair was long and straightened and dyed blonde.

I reached the car. But then it occurred to me – how was I going to get in without them seeing?

Then, to my horror, Mrs Turnbull whacked Lloyd round the back of the head, and to my astonishment, he started crying. I decided, on impulse, to take a chance. While their attention was elsewhere, I opened the back door, climbed in and closed it again. Neither

Lloyd Turnbull nor his mother seemed to notice. At that moment, the engine revved and the car rattled off down the road, smoke pumping from its exhaust.

CHAPTER TEN

I DISCOVER THAT I'M NOT INVISIBLE TO DOGS

The car fell into a tense, jagged silence. Mrs Turnbull took a cigarette out of a packet and lit it with a flip-up metal lighter. Her hair was not made of snakes and she wasn't all that bad looking, in a scorched sort of way – her face was red and raw but she had pretty hazel-coloured eyes and a pink mouth. All the same, I knew what Susan Brown meant about her being a gorgon. She had hardly stopped berating Lloyd Turnbull since he got in the car. Her voice was like one of the emery boards my mother used to file down her fingernails.

"What's the *point* of you?" she kept asking Lloyd Turnbull, as if he could possibly answer such a question. After all, what's the point of anyone?

The cigarette smoke was building up. All the windows were closed. I thought for a moment that I was going to start coughing, but I managed to suppress the urge.

I stared out of the window as we drove. At one point, I saw Mr Maurice Bailey drive by in his famous Land Rover. It was rusty, coughing great clouds of black smoke out into the atmosphere and making loud bangs. Attached to one wing there was a Union Jack flag, and he was driving too fast.

Eventually we pulled up outside what I presumed to be Lloyd Turnbull's residence. The block of flats was constructed from concrete, with a flat roof. It was the shape of a rectangle or cuboid. The concrete had discoloured with the weather so that there were long stains running down the front of the block.

There were perhaps twenty front doors in the block. The flats were on two levels and on the top level there was a narrow balcony or walkway. I waited and watched as Mrs Turnbull and Lloyd Archibald left the car and headed towards them. Mrs Turnbull walked in front, teetering on her high heels, and Lloyd Archibald followed behind, staring glumly at his feet. They entered a ground-floor flat and closed the door behind them. When I was sure no one was watching, I exited the vehicle.

I glanced up at the sky. It looked as if it was going to rain. I suddenly wondered whether, if it rained heavily, my body would be outlined by the precipitation that fell on me. I imagined that it would be. Then people would know I was invisible and I would lose my power.

Hurrying under the balcony that extended from the flats above, I was now faced with the problem of how to gain access to the Turnbulls' home. I could hardly ring on the doorbell and ask to be let in. I supposed I could get them to open the front door and then try to slip in, but it felt too risky.

I wondered if these places had gardens. I walked around the side of the building, out to the rear, and sure enough, there was an array of back yards. I counted the back doors until I came to the Turnbulls'. I saw an unsecured garden gate. On the other side a patch of bare, withered, untended lawn and plastic-framed French windows, covered by net curtains the colour of weak mustard.

I hurried up to the back door and tried the handle. The door was unlocked. I crept in as silently as I could. Although I didn't need to be all that quiet because Mrs Turnbull was shouting again.

There was mess and junk scattered around the place and clothes were strewn on the floor. Nothing was tidy. In the sink, there was a bowlful of washing-up on which dozens of flies had settled comfortably. The whole flat smelled of cigarettes and there were full ashtrays everywhere. There was a smell underneath the smoke – of old curry, processed food and chemical air freshener.

The door to the front room was open. I reached it just in time to see Mrs Turnbull grab Lloyd Archibald's withered arm and shake it, hard. He was wincing with pain. He could easily have knocked her over with his other, strong, arm, but he simply cowered.

"If Johnny was here to see this—" said Mrs Turnbull.

"If Dad was here, he wouldn't let you hit me," muttered Lloyd Turnbull. "But he couldn't stand the sight of you. He left because he fell in love with someone who was actually nice to him and didn't nag him all the time like a witch."

"Then why did he hardly ever come back to see you?"

"Because he was ill."

"He wasn't ill. He was a hopeless drunk. It was the drink that killed him. Or driving with half a pint of whisky inside him. Didn't do your arm much good either. What have you got to say about that? Your dad did that." She was still holding on to his bad arm. "Good dad, eh? A proper diamond."

There were tears in Lloyd Turnbull's eyes. "It wasn't half a pint, nothing like it. He wasn't drunk – it was an accident and it wasn't his fault. You're a bloody cow. I hate you. If Dad was still alive, things would be different."

"Too bad that he's dead then."

Then she shook his bad arm even harder and he almost doubled up in pain. I wanted to do something to stop her, but I couldn't. The woman seemed positively demented. She started screaming about all the effort she had made to give him a proper education, so that he could overcome being a "freak", and that this was how he repaid her.

Just then I froze with fear. A vicious-looking little dog had appeared in the doorway, barking as furiously as Mrs Turnbull was shouting. He was looking very fixedly in my direction. I supposed that he could smell me. He looked like he would enjoy nothing more than ripping my throat out and having my larynx for dinner. His whole body was like a clenched fist.

He took a step closer to me, and his barking became more frenetic. I was thinking about running, but I could never outpace him. I wondered if my blood was invisible because if it wasn't, it was going to make a hell of a mess on their carpet.

"Chronic, shut up!" said Mrs Turnbull, letting go of

Lloyd's arm and grabbing the animal fiercely by the collar.

"Now look what you've done," she said to Lloyd Turnbull. "You've upset my Popsicle."

At this, she got down on her knees and ruffled the back of the dog's neck, and then actually kissed him on the mouth. It was disgusting.

"He wants a walk," said Lloyd Turnbull, sullenly.

"If you think I'm going to fall for that one, you're mistaken. You're not taking him anywhere."

She turned towards the dog.

"You'll wake the dead, Chronic."

Chronic was looking at me as if he wanted to gnaw me to death. I knew he could smell me, and it felt as if he could see me. His barking got louder still as he strained at the collar. Mrs Turnbull fixed a choke chain to his neck and pulled on it as if to test it. She turned to Lloyd Turnbull.

"Go to your room and don't come out again. You're not getting anything to eat tonight. I'm taking Chronic out. He needs to do his business. Don't talk to me again. I don't want to hear your voice. I don't want to see your face. The sight of you makes me puke. You know why? Because it reminds me of your father. Get to your room. Go on, before I lose my rag completely."

Lloyd Turnbull didn't move. He just stood staring at his mother with absolute hatred in his eyes. Mrs Turnbull pulled the choke chain tight, so Chronic's bark suddenly became a strained whimper. Lloyd Turnbull looked at Chronic, who now seemed to be having trouble breathing. Mrs Turnbull pulled the choke chain even tighter, and Chronic appeared to stop breathing altogether.

"Go to your room," said Mrs Turnbull again, this time very quietly.

Slowly, resentfully, Lloyd Turnbull turned and walked towards the rear of the flat without another word.

Seconds later, Mrs Turnbull left with the dog and the house fell into a melancholy silence.

Very carefully, I traced Lloyd Turnbull's steps to his bedroom. The door was open a crack. I dared not open it further. But looking through, I could see Lloyd Archibald Turnbull doing something very strange.

He was punching his bad arm with the fist of his good arm, over and over again, so hard that it must have left bruises.

Then he stopped, reached over and shut the door with such a bang that I jumped.

I just stood there for a while and examined my feelings. I didn't feel at all triumphant despite all the hard times that Lloyd Turnbull had given me. All I was aware of was sadness – his sadness.

I looked at my watch. The Turnbulls didn't live far from us and if I hurried home, I might still have a chance to catch Melchior and Peaches having their Big Conversation. I left the flat the same way I had come in. Back out on the main street, I snuck into an Indian restaurant which had a full-length mirror, restored myself to visibility and hurried home as fast as I could.

Peaches had not come back from pilates yet, and Melchior was sitting in a chair reading *New Scientist* magazine. When he heard me come in, he looked up from the magazine and smiled.

"Strato, is everything OK? You look a bit out of breath. Have you been running? Sit down. Would you like a glass of water?"

I said I would. Melchior stood up and ruffled my hair. That's the other thing he does, along with tapping me on the nose. He sniffed the air.

"You smell of curry."

"We had it for lunch at school today."

"Not according to the menu we've got pinned up on the fridge."

Melchior has an acute memory. It can be quite irritating.

"It's out of date."

"What kind of curry was it?"

"Dad, I'm thirsty."

"Sorry, Fender."

Fender is his pet name for me, after "Fender Stratocaster" – a make of guitar. I sat down and Melchior went to fetch me the water.

My father is a very nice man, although often somewhat abstracted. He is so absent-minded that on one occasion he forgot to put his swimming trunks on at the public swimming baths and emerged from the changing rooms totally naked. I don't know how he felt about it, but I had never been so embarrassed in my life.

All the same, Melchior is a good father. When I was younger, Melchior was always the one to read to me in bed, and take me to the park to play football. Peaches cooked and fussed and liked a good hug, but my father did all the fun stuff. I thought it was terrible that Lloyd Archibald Turnbull only had that gorgon to look after him.

My father returned and handed me a glass of water with ice in it.

"Is that OK? Do you want anything else? I've put some lamb chops on the griddle for your supper."

I nodded and smiled, worrying about the lamb chops. Melchior went back to reading, and – partly because I was now used to being invisible – I just sat there and watched him as if he couldn't see me.

I watched the way his crinkly forehead gave way to thinning browny-grey hair, and the laughter lines around his eyes, and his soft, rather full-lipped mouth, which always looked like it was about to break into a smile. I *did* like Melchior very much. In fact, it wouldn't be an exaggeration to say that he was my hero.

He looked up, catching me in mid-examination, and grinned.

"Beam me up, Scotty," he said.

I smiled. "Why do you want me to beam you up?"

"Because you're staring at me. It's a bit discomfiting."

"Discomfiting", incidentally, means "causing unease or embarrassment".

"I was just daydreaming and you were in my eye-line," I said.

"Good. I would be worried if I thought you found me all that interesting."

"No. I don't. No need to worry."

Now it was his turn to stare at me – kindly, but intently. Eventually he said, "I hear you got into trouble at school today. Dr Ojebande left a message on the answering machine to say that you would be late."

"I'm sorry. Yes, I was kept back. I called Peaches to let

her know. Didn't she tell you?"

"She'd already left when I got back from work. Maybe she left a note. I didn't see it though."

"I was five minutes late for his lesson, because I had an upset stomach. He gave me an hour's detention."

"Do you think he was picking on you?" asked Melchior, heading for the kitchen.

"I do think so, yes," I replied.

"'Is it cos I's black?'" he said, in a mock ghetto voice. He always does this when he's trying to be funny, impersonating that old comedian, Ali G, from the television. "Seriously though – do you think he was singling you out?"

He was making a salad to go with the lamb chops. Even he couldn't ruin a salad. The lamb chops were a different matter.

"No, I don't think so," I said. "Dr Ojebande is also black."

Melchior nodded. "I thought you were the only one in this hick town."

"Apparently not," I replied, enjoying the smell of the seared lamb chops before my father burnt them.

He turned to me. "Honestly though, Strato. Do you like it here? Are you OK? Because it's very different from London, isn't it?"

I hesitated, wondering whether to tell the truth or not.

"I don't mind it," I said finally. "I'll get used to it."

Melchior looked dubious.

"And they do have a very good ice-cream shop," I added.

"That's true," said Melchior, nodding as he tossed the

salad. "But is a good ice-cream shop enough to make you live somewhere?"

I had learned a thing or two about how to avoid answering difficult questions by now.

"Are *you* happy here, Melchior?"

Melchior took the salad out of the bowl and put it on a plate with a slice of wholemeal bread.

"I know that your mother and I have our problems, but on the whole I like it here. Yes, I'm happy enough."

I nodded and thought to myself, *I shall see how true that is in about two hours time.*

I turned towards the cooker, from where clouds of smoke were billowing.

"I think the chops are burning, Father."

They were.

Melchior was lying about being happy. When I made myself invisible and crept downstairs later that night and hid in the corner of the front room again, I found out all about the situation between my parents.

There were no meals in front of the telly this time. Instead, Melchior and Peaches sat facing one another across the table that stands against the wall opposite the bay windows. They each had a large glass of red wine and very serious expressions on their faces.

I won't tell you everything that was said. To be honest, it was all so shocking, I do not really remember the words. All I could think was how silly I had been to think I could do anything about it. And how close to the edge Peaches and Melchior really were, and that if they fell into the abyss, I would fall with them. Then perhaps

I would be like Lloyd Archibald Turnbull, with only one parent, missing the other all the time.

At the heart of the problem, it turned out, was the fact that my father hadn't resigned his job just because my mother had wanted to move to Hedgecombe. He had resigned his job because he had been having a "relationship" with a young woman called Annabel at his research laboratory. Apparently she was only twenty-three years old.

"Relationship" was not the word Peaches used. The word she used was much worse.

Peaches, it seemed, had found out about the relationship and as a consequence had insisted that they move away from London and as far away from this woman as possible. From what I could glean, Peaches had always wanted to live in the countryside anyway, and as an aspiring author, Hedgecombe-upon-Dray with its literary heritage appealed to her in particular. As penance for his impropriety, Melchior had agreed to give up his job and move away.

It seemed that Melchior had had little choice in the matter. It had been ship out to Hedgecombe or "this relationship is going up the wazoo," to use Peaches' less-than-poetic phrase.

I didn't know what a wazoo was, but I guessed that it wasn't a good place for a relationship to end up.

The point Melchior made vociferously and on several occasions that evening was that *I* had been punished because of *his* bad behaviour. I had been taken away from my school and friends, for instance. But Peaches had been positively glad for me to leave the school and enter the mainstream education system. She thought it would "socialize" me.

I got progressively more upset as the conversation went on. But the worst was still to come. Because there was another bone of contention between Melchior and Peaches. It turned out to be the mystery book that my mother was writing.

It seemed that my mother's book was not a novel, as I had always imagined. It was a non-fiction book about the difficulties of being the parent of a gifted and talented child.

The title of the book was *Welcome to the Geek Farm*, and she had now signed a deal with the publisher Dorothea Beckwith-Hinds worked for.

My father, I learned, opposed my mother writing this book. He said that it would be harmful to me, and would invade my privacy. My mother responded by saying that she would, in due course, seek my approval, and anyway, it was her first and possibly only chance to be published and why couldn't he care about her for once?

To which Melchior replied that it was because I was his son and it would upset me, which I thought was a good reply. But Peaches said that if he was so fond of his son, he shouldn't have gone screwing around.

Melchior said that I was too young to be asked to approve or veto a project like this from my mother, and that even making me aware of its existence could hurt my feelings. He also pointed out that I might well give my approval even though I did not want to, out of a desire for her approbation. And furthermore, I wasn't old enough to be aware of the possible consequences of such a book.

I should emphasize that this discussion did not proceed in a calm and orderly way. Voices were repeatedly raised, and tempers were severely frayed. Melchior's temporary walk-out a few days previously seemed to indicate that he was already at the end of his tether, even though we had only been in Hedgecombe for a few weeks. Peaches, it appeared, interpreted this as him wishing to return to London to reunite with his lover.

Melchior replied that she hadn't been his lover, merely someone he had had sex with on two occasions, and that he did not love her, that he loved Peaches and me. Peaches meanwhile insisted that he had betrayed her and that what he had done was unforgivable. Melchior replied that what she was doing with the book was equally unforgivable.

Then they fell into an awkward silence. Nothing, it appeared, had been achieved other than the airing of negative emotions.

Oddly enough, after I snuck back up to my room that night and made myself visible again, I felt better. Somehow, knowing what was at the heart of all the tension in the house made it easier to bear. I realized that it really wasn't my fault after all. It was Melchior's and Peaches' fault, in equal measure as far as I could calculate. It had nothing to do with me whatsoever. That was a relief.

I must admit, I was taken aback by my mother's intention to write the book, particularly by the implication of the title. As for my father's indiscretion, what I found remarkable was that any young woman – even a "slut", as

127

my mother preferred to describe her – could have found him attractive in the first place. Thinning hair, somewhat pot-bellied, stoop-shouldered and ancient – forty-one years old – he struck me as an unlikely Lothario. However, it had been a pretty cheap trick to play on my mother, and now that I'd had time to think about it I was quite angry with him. But I knew that my father was a good and kind man. I supposed that he was flawed too – but then, who isn't? Even heroes have their weaknesses.

CHAPTER ELEVEN

THE HAUNTING OF MRS AMBER TURNBULL

On Monday morning, I rose early – I didn't want to be late again. In fact, I got up too early. I was left with about half an hour with nothing to do before leaving to catch the bus. I found myself daydreaming. I thought this sentence to myself: *Time is really dragging.* Then I started to think about time.

The expression "time is relative" is used colloquially to suggest that sometimes your *perception* of time is relative – sometimes it seems to go slowly, and sometimes it seems to go fast. But time really is relative. It's elastic – it stretches and contracts.

If I jumped in a spaceship and headed for the nearest star, which (other than the Sun) is Alpha Centauri – about five light years away – and travelled there at close to the speed of light, then turned round and came back again, I would be ten years older when I arrived back on Earth. But the people I had left behind on Earth – Melchior, Peaches, Lloyd Archibald Turnbull and Dr Ojebande, for example – would not be ten years older.

They would either be very old or dead of old age. A lot more time would have passed for them than for me.

This is not a theory, but a solid, experimentally proven fact. The closer you travel to the speed of light, the slower time goes for you – at least that's the way it is for someone who *isn't* travelling at close to the speed of light, which includes everyone on Earth.

People on Earth are only travelling at a little more than 1,600 kilometres per hour, which is the speed at which the Earth rotates on its axis. Or perhaps they are travelling at 108,000 kilometres per hour, which is the speed that the Earth goes round the Sun.

That's the point, you see – you can only describe how fast you are going by having something to compare it to.

The only absolute in the universe is the speed of light. This never varies, which is thoroughly weird and magical. Let me give an example of how weird and magical it is.

Imagine you are driving a car along a road at 40 kilometres per hour.

Now imagine that, 80 kilometres away at the opposite end of the road, your father starts driving a car towards you at 40 kilometres per hour.

How long before you and your father reach one another?

Your speed, as far as you are concerned, is 40 kilometres per hour. That is the speed you are travelling at relative to the road. Your father is travelling at the same speed, 40 kilometres per hour, relative to the road.

You are travelling directly towards each other. So *relative to one another* your speed is 80 kilometres per hour.

Therefore, since you are 80 kilometres apart, you and your father will reach each other in precisely one hour.

Now imagine two laser-beam torches on the same road, 80 kilometres apart.

Imagine that the speed of light is 40 kilometres per hour (which obviously it isn't, but bear with me).

You and your father are each standing next to one of these torches.

Imagine that, instead of travelling in a car, you and your father have the ability to ride on the solid beams of light that come from the laser torches.

Then, at exactly the same moment, someone switches the two torches on.

How long will it take you to reach one another?

Obviously the same amount of time as it would take if you travelled by car. One hour, right?

Wrong. It will take two hours.

Because the speed of light is not relative. It is *always the same*.

Of course, light does not travel at 40 kilometres per hour. It travels at 300,000 kilometres per second.

So now you have to imagine that you and your father are standing not 80, but 300,000 kilometres away from one another on a very, very long road.

Let's say you both set off on a journey towards one another on a *real* beam of light.

Each light beam will be travelling towards the other at 600,000 kilometres per second relative to one another.

Therefore, you would pass each other in precisely half of one second flat. Right?

Wrong. Because the speed of light *is not relative*.

So it will still take a whole second to travel 300,000 kilometres even though each light beam is travelling at 300,000 kilometres per second towards one another.

Because nothing can travel faster than a beam of light, not even two beams of light relative to one another.

Although they are travelling towards each other at 300,000 kilometres per second, their speed, relative to one another, is *still* only 300,000 kilometres per second.

It makes no sense – it's impossible – but it's a proven fact. I don't know why it's true, and I don't know why it means that time slows down as you go faster. I haven't worked out the relationship between light and time, and perhaps I never will. But it's something to do with time and space being flip sides of the same thing – which is why it's called "space-time" – in the same way that matter and energy, and electricity and magnetism, are two sides of the same thing.

I don't think I will ever be clever enough to understand how the universe works. It's just too big, extraordinary and super-weird.

These were the random thoughts that were skittering like spilt marbles through my head as I was waiting to leave my house that morning. Other teenagers daydream about scoring a goal in the World Cup Final. I dream about the peculiarity of the universe. Which makes me peculiar too, no doubt.

I glanced up at the clock on the wall. Time, even if it is relative in Einstein's physics, appears to be absolute in Hedgecombe-upon-Dray. No negotiation is possible.

I was late. I had been lost in my own little world for so long, I now had to run for the bus.

I got a fresh surprise when I ran out of the door towards the bus stop. There was a small figure with a curtain of hair and pink-rimmed spectacles standing there.

It was Susan Brown.

I wasn't sure what to do. I had made my mind up by now that Susan Brown was in cahoots with Lloyd Archibald Turnbull. But really there was nothing I could bloody well do. Unless I wanted to miss the bus, I would have to go and stand at the bus stop with her.

She watched me meditatively as I approached. She fiddled with her glasses, then took them off for a moment, and then replaced them. It occurred to me once again that, glasses on or off, she was terribly pretty. Her face was so nice it seemed hard to believe that she could be friends with Lloyd Turnbull.

But my scientific training had enabled me to grasp the principle that reality is often not what it seems.

I looked down the road, desperately hoping for the bus to arrive. It was nowhere in sight.

I asked for Scotty to beam me up but, as usual, he did not oblige. So rather reluctantly, I went and stood about a metre away from Susan Brown.

We stood there in silence for several seconds. Then, eventually, she spoke.

"Are you angry with me, Strato Nyman?"

I mumbled that I wasn't. This was not true. I was just too intimidated to speak my mind.

I hated being shy. I wondered if it was my personality, or if something was wrong with my biochemistry.

It can happen. In the nineteenth century there was an illness called erethism, which hat-makers used to suffer from. It came from mercury poisoning, and it made you pathologically timid and lacking in self-confidence. Perhaps I was suffering from a modern version of erethism.

She studied my face through her spectacle lenses.

"Strato? You *are* – aren't you? Why are you angry with me?"

Suddenly, without warning, I felt exhausted. My shoulders slumped. I realized, there and then, that I was worn out with the effort of being shy. Then my exhaustion was replaced by anger. Obviously, hearing my parents fight the night before had had a bigger effect on me than I had imagined. Something was bottled up inside me and I needed to let it out.

"Because you're just another bloody liar!" I blurted.

I could hardly believe what I had just said.

Susan Brown took a step backwards. Then the words started to tumble out. I couldn't stop myself.

"You pretend to be nice to me, and then you hang about with Lloyd Turnbull. Just like Turnbull pretends to be nice to me and then uses it against me. At least Dr Ojebande doesn't pretend to like me. I don't know what's wrong with people down here in the countryside. Why are you so nasty? I haven't done anything wrong. I'm sick of it. What is the matter with everyone? What is the matter with *you*, Susan Brown? Whose side are you on anyway?"

Just as suddenly as it had arrived, the anger dissipated, like smoke from a damped-down fire. I felt ashamed and embarrassed, but at the same time it was as if a weight had lifted from me.

Susan Brown was struck dumb. Her mouth hung open slightly. I looked down at the ground, already regretting that I had spoken out.

At that moment, the bus pulled up next to us. The doors opened and I hurried inside.

Mr Maurice Bailey was grinning as usual.

"You alright, Robertson?"

I looked round to see who he was talking to, but there was only Susan Brown behind me. I ignored Mr Maurice Bailey and went and sat down on an empty two-person seat by myself.

I watched Susan Brown arguing with Mr Bailey about something or other. She seemed to be getting very frustrated, but Mr Bailey was just laughing. Eventually she made her way up the bus, her face red. To my surprise, she sat next to me.

"He shouldn't have that job," she said, nodding towards Mr Bailey.

I didn't know what Susan Brown was talking about. Mr Bailey had always seemed perfectly nice to me, even if he did make weird comments.

She stared ahead of her. It seemed she was as angry as I had been. Then suddenly she turned to me.

"I don't know how you could say all those bad things about me. I hate Lloyd Turnbull. I didn't choose to sit next to him on Friday. Dr Ojebande sat him there because he thought it might make him behave better. There's no reason for you to be nasty to me. I've never said anything bad to you, have I?"

Now she was looking at me. I could feel myself blushing.

"Well? Have I, Strato Nyman?"

Now that I thought about it, she hadn't. Then I remembered Dr Ojebande talking about Lloyd Turnbull being "re-seated".

Maybe she was telling the truth. Perhaps she was on my side, after all. But I was scared to trust her. So I didn't say anything and we sat in silence.

Then, after a few more minutes had passed, she said – in a different kind of voice, softer and more friendly – "You're very good at science, aren't you?"

"I just like it a lot," I replied, meek as a kitten again.

She nodded. Then – this was where the big surprise came – she said, "I like it too. It's like magic, isn't it? Real-life magic."

Now I was flummoxed. I really wanted to believe she was not a secret agent for Lloyd Turnbull and the two Waynes but I still couldn't be sure. I looked at her. Her face seemed soft and open.

"Yes," I said. "Yes, it is like magic."

Susan Brown nodded again. "I'm a bit of a science nerd myself," she said.

"I prefer to think of myself as a geek," I said.

She laughed – a lovely tinkling sound – then she nodded as if she understood completely.

"I'm not as good at it as you are, but I think it's really interesting. I've got some science programmes on the Sky⁺ box back at home. Did you see that documentary about chaos theory that was on last week?"

I hadn't seen it. I had wanted to, but Melchior had

forgotten to press the record button on our Sky⁺ box. I'd been meaning to watch it on iPlayer, but I hadn't got round to it.

I couldn't believe that Susan Brown had seen it. And if she was just pretending to be friendly, then she was an excellent actress who had done an awful lot of research.

"No," I said. "It looked really interesting."

She seemed to hesitate before saying, "Would you like to come to my house sometime and watch it?"

I gulped, took a deep breath and said, "Me?"

Which was a stupid thing to say, but she just smiled and said, "Yes, you. Who do you think?"

Then the bus arrived at the school and we all piled out.

I couldn't concentrate on my lessons that day. I kept thinking about Susan Brown and how rude I'd been to her, and Lloyd Archibald Turnbull and the look of pain on his face when his mother had shaken his arm.

It hadn't just been physical pain, I could tell that. It had been emotional hurt. He had lost his father, and he had a mother who was obviously abusive. It was no wonder that he behaved so aggressively. Sometimes, my father used to say, being angry is just another way of being sad. That night, I decided to do something about it.

At around midnight, when my parents were fast asleep, I put on my clothes, then I took the book and jumped into the mirror.

I had decided to take two things with me. I had them in my pockets when I jumped.

One of my favourite gifts from my thirteenth birthday

was an electronic voice changer. When you spoke into it, it altered the sound waves of your voice so that you talked like a robot, or an alien, or a witch, or a demon.

It was fun, although both Melchior and Peaches had got irritated with it quite quickly, since I started using it almost all the time, sometimes waking them at six in the morning with a loud alien commentary on their laziness at remaining in bed. Eventually they took the batteries out and hid them. Then I bought some more batteries, so they hid the voice changer. But I found it.

The other thing I had in my pocket was an eight-ounce piece of prime rump steak.

I was worried about Chronic. I was hoping he would be asleep. If he wasn't, I would just have to leg it and go back another night. With any luck, the steak might distract him long enough for me to get away.

It worked in *Tom and Jerry* cartoons, anyway.

The Turnbulls' flat was only fifteen minutes' walk away. I didn't see a soul on the way there.

All the lights in their flat were out, and I made my way carefully and silently along the back alleyway.

I was gambling that the back door was going to be unlocked like before. It was. I crept in, picking my way through the debris. It seemed they had eaten fish and chips for supper, because the flat still smelled of salt and vinegar and there were discarded paper cones on the floor.

On the table was a letter addressed to "Mrs Amber Turnbull". That gave me another useful piece of information – Mrs Turnbull's Christian name. I made my way to what I assumed to be her bedroom. There was no sound from Chronic.

In her room, Mrs Amber Turnbull was snoring, loudly. Her dyed blonde hair was spread out on the pillow and her body moved up and down with her breathing. Her left arm protruded from the bedclothes and I could see that she was wearing pink pyjamas with little blue roses on. The room smelled of chemical air freshener and cigarettes, but unlike the other rooms in the flat, it was tidy. There were stuffed toys and teddy bears on the chair by the side of the bed.

I considered the problem of how to wake her up. There was a glass full of water next to her. I thought I would take the direct route.

I emptied it over her head.

She immediately sat up straight, her eyes trying to focus. She was mumbling swear words. I raised the voice changer to my mouth. I had adjusted it to the setting marked "Witch". It made my voice seem high and cracked and terrifying.

"Amber," I said. "This is Johnny."

She actually screamed. Her eyes widened more than you would have imagined possible – they were completely round. She froze stock still. I could actually see goosebumps rise on her scrawny arms. I now saw that on her left arm she had a tattoo of a dagger behind a red heart. There was an arrow going through the heart and blood dripping from the dagger and arrow tips. The caption read "True Love", but it looked more like it represented a threat.

"I saw you hit the boy," I continued. "You shouldn't have done it."

Still Mrs Turnbull didn't speak. She had gone very pale.

From downstairs, rather worryingly, I could hear the sound of frenetic barking.

Mrs Turnbull was shivering and looking around her wildly. I thought I could smell a sweet, sickly toilet smell in the air, which the air freshener was incapable of covering up.

"You leave him alone," I said, now whispering into the mic, which gave my voice an even more sinister sound. "You treat him like a mother should."

All that poor Mrs Turnbull could manage was a faint nod. I thought she was going to be sick on the floor. Her face was the colour of porridge.

I heard the sound of little feet pounding up the stairs. The barking became fiercer. I felt in my pocket for the piece of steak. Suddenly it seemed a very forlorn hope that it would distract Chronic if he was in full flood.

"You hit him again, and I'll be back. Then you'll be sorry. I promise."

Now it was time to get to the point.

"Something else. He's been bullying other boys. Particularly one called Strato Nyman. N. Y. M. A. N. Nyman. You've got to stop him picking on that boy or I'm coming back."

I switched the voice distorter to "Demon" for greater effect. It got lower and creepier.

"He's bullying other kids because you're bullying him. Both of you had better stop."

She nodded, wide-eyed.

I raised the voice changer to my mouth again. I could hear Chronic scratching at the door. I looked at the window to see if I would have a chance of jumping out of it. There probably wouldn't be time – it was secured tight with a window lock.

"Amber. Listen to me. What's the name of the boy that our Lloyd has been bullying?"

"S … S … Strato. Strato N … Norman."

"Strato *Nyman*, you muppet."

"Nyman."

"Don't you forget it."

She shook her head desperately.

At that moment, the door swung open. I reached for the steak in my left-hand pocket, as Chronic's barking reached hysterical proportions.

To my relief, Lloyd Turnbull was standing there, holding him by the collar.

"Mum," he said. "What's wrong?"

Then I watched with pleasure as Mrs Amber Turnbull fainted, flat out on her bed. She didn't look peaceful either. She looked absolutely terrified.

While Lloyd Turnbull held the dog, I rushed out of the open door. Chronic barked worse than ever, but Lloyd held him tightly. I was through the back door in a flash.

As I made my way home, I imagined that Lloyd Turnbull's life was about to take a turn for the better. Mine too, with any luck.

Back indoors, I returned the steak to the fridge. It would have been a shame to waste it, even if Melchior only ended up burning it.

CHAPTER TWELVE

A DRONE, A GNOME
AND A VICTORIA SPONGE

The next morning, I woke up with the first verse of a song by The Smiths going round and round my head.

Shyness is nice and
Shyness can stop you
From doing all the things in life
You'd like to

The song seemed to be speaking to me. So when I saw Susan Brown on the bus again, I plucked up my courage and told her I could come over that night to watch the TV programme, if she still wanted me to.

She smiled, and said that was fine and should we travel home on the bus together? I felt myself blushing again – this was beginning to feel like a "date" rather than two people arranging to watch a science programme together.

Perhaps if it was a date, that wasn't such a bad thing. Maybe Susan Brown would try and kiss me. I had never kissed a girl before, and it seemed like it would be an intellectually interesting experience.

I was probably getting carried away. She was just being friendly – actually, she was the only person who had been friendly to me in all the time I'd been at Whitecross.

I rang Peaches at lunchtime and told her I was going to a friend's house after school. She seemed a little surprised, but quite pleased.

"You're going where?"

"To Susan Brown's house."

"Who's Susan Brown?"

"A girl at school."

"Really?"

"Really."

"Well – you've been a busy bee, haven't you, genius?" She cackled when she said this. My mother has a nice cackle, like a good witch. "You sly fox. Is she pretty?"

"I don't really want to discuss this any more, Mother. I will be home at about nine o'clock I expect."

"She is, isn't she? I bet she is. I'd love to meet her. Why don't you bring her back to our house sometime?"

"I think that would be premature."

She started cackling again.

"Premature, eh? That's a good one. OK, fine, dahlin'. Whatever you say. Have a good time. And don't do anything I wouldn't."

"What does that mean?"

"Never mind, never mind. Tell me all about it later. Tell me everything."

"Goodbye, Mother."

"Goodbye, Strato. But aren't you a dark horse."

"Well, which am I? A horse, a fox or a bee? Or some other species?"

"Maybe you're a love cat."

Then she made a noise like a cat purring – "Rrrrr."

She gave one final cackle and then put the phone down, leaving me considerably discomfited and determined never to mention anything to my mother about me and Susan Brown again. The way she went on about it, it was as if we were about to get married or something. She was being typically immature.

Nothing much happened at school that afternoon. I kept a careful eye on Lloyd Turnbull. He was unusually well-behaved. I was struggling to carry on disliking him after visiting his home again the previous night. I felt sorry for him. Clearly having an abusive mother and a dead father wasn't much fun.

The journey home with Susan Brown was quite enjoyable. We got talking at last, properly. She had this knack for drawing me out of my shell. It turned out she really *was* a science geek. She was actually more into biology than physics and she told me some amazing things about the human body that I had never realized.

One of the oddest things she told me was that cells in the body are renewing themselves all the time, and at the end of seven years, or thereabouts, you do not have a single cell in your body that was the same as it was before that time. Physically, you are a completely newly grown person every seven years. Yet you *are* the same – same build, same hair colour, same face, same personality. It struck me as utterly bizarre.

I had to counter that. I couldn't let her come up with

more interesting facts than me. So I told her about the conservation of matter, which is sort of the reverse of the fact that a body changes every seven years. Because although the stuff that makes up a body changes, the stuff that makes up the universe does not – ever.

In fact, the universe has not changed since the microsecond in which it was born.

This is what the conservation of matter means. It's another boring name for an incredible thing – the fact that not a single atom has been destroyed or created since the universe began fifteen billion years ago.

The atoms that make up you and me and your supper and everything else were forged in the Big Bang. Those atoms that are in your table and your computer and your hamster were, at other times, people fighting battles in ancient Greece, buildings in Rome, sandals in Egypt.

Civilizations have risen and fallen, people have lived and died – but it's all exactly the same stuff that's doing it and that it's happening to. Nothing is ever destroyed and nothing is ever created.

That's what the conservation of matter means – that the universe is immortal and, in a way, so are we. All atoms do is rearrange themselves into different forms over and over again as the universe moves through time. They might become mud, then a leaf, then a knife, then a person, then mud again, then a dragonfly. This endless reshuffling goes on forever.

The bus pulled up at the bus stop past mine, and we got out at Susan Brown's house.

Her house was lovely. It was an old stone cottage with ivy covering the front wall. Susan said it was eighteenth century. It actually had a real thatched roof and leaded windows. The door was old, gnarled, plain wood, and even though it was autumn, the front garden was full of colour and life. Instead of being tidy and geometrical like our garden, it was beautifully chaotic, with flowers, vines and bushes fighting one another for space.

Susan let herself in the front door. I heard a woman's voice say, "Hello," and Susan say, "Hello, Mum – I've got a friend with me."

The front room, like the outside of the house, was highly appealing. My father and mother have never had a great deal of aesthetic sensibility, shopping largely at IKEA and pound shops, but this was something else. Everything looked old, but not old and worn out, just lived in and shiny, warm and comfortable. There was a huge overstuffed sofa, oil paintings and watercolours on the walls – I think they were real, and not just prints – nice oriental rugs and polished walnutty tables and chests of drawers. Two of the walls were entirely covered with books from floor to ceiling.

Then Susan's mother walked in. Usually, in Hedgecombe, when people met me for the first time, I could tell that they were slightly taken aback by the fact that I am black, if only for a moment. They flinched slightly, or their eyes darted momentarily off to the side. It didn't mean that they were racially prejudiced. I think they were just taken by surprise.

Mrs Brown didn't do that. She didn't give any sign of noticing that I was different at all. She simply gave me a lovely smile and welcomed me, and said, "So you're the famous Strato Nyman!" as if Susan was always talking about me. Then she introduced herself as Xanthe – pronounced Zan-thee – and asked me if I would like some fresh lemonade and Victoria sponge cake. I did not demur.

She was a handsome woman, maybe 1.75 metres with grey hair tied back behind her head, and she wore blue jeans and a sloppy T-shirt that read: "The Sports Team from My Area is Superior to the Sports Team from Your Area". I think this was meant to be satirical. Then she said, "My, you're a handsome boy, aren't you?" and Susan told her to shut up, but in a nice way, and she laughed and went off to get our lemonade and cake.

Susan and I sat down and carried on chatting about science. She told me she was particularly interested in biology because she loved animals. At that moment, a small cocker spaniel ran in from a side door and jumped up and licked her face. I said I liked dogs, but my parents would not let me have one.

She said animals were lovely, but then we were just animals too. Then she said, did I know that we shared most of our genes with fruit flies and about half of them with tomatoes? I laughed because it seemed funny somehow. Geek humour, I suppose. She laughed too – that lovely, soft, tinkling sound. It was what I imagined a cloud of butterflies taking flight with tiny bells attached to their wings might sound like.

Mrs Brown brought in the lemonade and the cake, both of which were home-made and delicious. Then we watched the documentary on chaos theory, something I had read about but did not really understand.

I'm not sure I understood it much more after watching

the programme either. It described how chaos theory grew out of the study of stuff like mayonnaise, i.e. molecules that stick together in an almost jelly-like way.

The presenter talked about the great scientist Alan Turing, who came up with the idea that organisms might be governed by mathematical regularities in the same way that crystals and rocks are.

Things as wobbly and strange and uneven as people, hamsters and goldfish could have been made through a random accident over billions of years, becoming ordered without anyone in control. The fundamental mathematical structure of the universe organized everything to its own "plan".

That is chaos theory. It is not about chaos at all, but the opposite, in a way – how an incredible level of organization emerges automatically out of disorder, simply because of certain mathematical rules that take on the role of God, making everything happen in a certain way. Like I said, I didn't understand it, really – but I did enjoy trying to understand it.

After the documentary, Susan's father arrived home and he was quite as nice as Mrs Xanthe Brown – tall, broad-shouldered, good-looking and with a gleaming smile. His name was Euan and he had an Irish accent. We all ate dinner together and I felt like I was part of their family – they were so nice and friendly and intelligent. The food was something sweet and meaty and ricey and fruity called a tagine. It certainly beat Melchior's burnt lamb chops and death-mushroom omelettes.

After dinner, me and Susan decided to stop being science nerds. We got some popcorn and went to Susan's room and watched a completely non-scientific movie – one that I'd seen before and really loved, called *Rat Race*. The story is about six teams of people given the task of racing 563 miles (918 kilometres) from a Las Vegas casino to a train station in Silver City, New Mexico, trying to be the first to reach a storage locker containing two million dollars. It had John Cleese in it and Rowan Atkinson and Whoopi Goldberg. I had really never had such a lovely time. We laughed so much at one point we could barely speak, and I thought I might die because I couldn't catch my breath.

When nine o'clock came, I said I thought I ought to be getting home, although I didn't really want to go at all, but I thought my mother and father might be worrying about me. So I put my jacket on, and all three of them saw me to the door, and just as I was leaving, Susan Brown leaned over and gave me a little kiss on the cheek.

I felt that must be what it was like to drink champagne. I blushed, and went home feeling happier than I had done for years.

A few weeks later, we had a day off school – it was a teacher training day. Although it was now mid-October, the weather was bizarrely warm – 25 degrees Celsius. It wasn't a record but it was pretty hot for late autumn.

It would turn out to be the last summery day of the year. My mother was working on her book, squirrelled away in her study, but my father, as usual, had to go to work. I could never understand why he didn't want me coming to his laboratory. He always blamed health and safety regulations.

So, on impulse, I decided to join him. Not that he was going to know anything about it.

I told Melchior and Peaches I was going into Hedgecombe to tour the bookshops. Then I slipped upstairs, got hold of the book, took a running jump at the mirror and hurried outside, just in time to climb into the back of my dad's car before he headed off to work.

I was looking forward to seeing his new laboratory. The old one, which had been at a university, had been full of exciting technology – a scintillation detector, a particle accelerator and electron microscopes, and there had been rumours of quantum computers hidden away in secret rooms. I wasn't sure what all these machines were for, but they had certainly looked exciting, and the fact that Melchior knew how they worked and was in charge of them had made me feel proud of him and proud that I was his son.

Now I was going to see his new laboratory. I wondered why Melchior did not want me to visit his workplace. I didn't believe his health and safety regulations excuse for a moment, but I had no idea what the real reason was. Perhaps he was involved in secret government projects and had signed the Official Secrets Act. Whatever the reason, I thought that so long as I kept out of the way, and so long as they didn't have an invisible-boy detector set up, I would be fine.

After about ten minutes in the car, we drew to a stop. I was surprised at the building we parked outside. My father's old laboratory had been on a university campus, surrounded by fine and elegant buildings, and his office had been capacious and well-furnished. This building looked not all that dissimilar to the block of flats that Lloyd Archibald Turnbull lived in. It was grey and ugly, with small windows and an ordinary-sized front door. I followed Melchior as he exited the car and made his way towards it. A plastic sign outside read: "Department of Science and Technology".

Melchior let himself in with a card key, and I followed him into a hall, then a corridor, where he paused to buy a cup of coffee from a machine, and finally into a small, cupboard-like room with no natural light in it. I wondered why he was going in there, until I realized, with a shock, that it was his office. It was half the size of the old one and much uglier.

He unpacked his papers. He sat down in the chair. He switched on his computer. And then he just stayed there, staring at the screen and sipping his grey-looking coffee.

After a while, I decided to wander around the building looking for the laboratory, but it wasn't that big a building, and after about twenty minutes I was absolutely sure that there was nothing of the kind. On the way back to Melchior's office, I saw the sign: "Clerical Staff This Way".

And then, slowly but irrevocably, the awful truth dawned on me.

My father's new job didn't involve him being a scientist at all. He was simply an administrative worker in a government department now. He shuffled paper. He rearranged paper clips.

He was a bloody drone.

This was what Peaches had done to him by forcing

him to move away from London.

Stunned, I ran out of the building at top speed. I very nearly bumped into a party of young people waiting for a bus outside the building, I was so distracted.

I felt empty and confused. I didn't know who to turn to. I needed to share this with someone. But who?

I summoned up my courage and decided to call Susan Brown. She had said we could go swimming if the weather was good. But she wasn't answering her phone.

I wandered purposelessly, not knowing what else to do with myself. Of all the things I had learned since I started to become invisible, this was the hardest to bear. I was angry but not sure who to be angry with and why. Peaches for making Melchior leave his job? Melchior for sleeping with someone else and bringing this situation about? Melchior for lying to me? The blaming business was a very complicated one, I was discovering.

I was so caught up in my thoughts, I nearly bumped into someone else, but just skipped out of the way in time. I needed to get visible again, or I was in danger of being found out.

I glanced up to see who I had nearly collided with. To my surprise, it was Mr Maurice Bailey the bus driver. It was a small town, Hedgecombe. He had clearly just been shopping as he was carrying two bulging plastic supermarket bags.

He was heading out of town, where there were no crowds to put me in danger. I decided to follow him home. Susan Brown had suggested that Mr Bailey was perhaps not quite as friendly as he seemed. He clearly needed investigating. Also, it would keep my mind occupied as it snapped and snarled around the discovery that my father wasn't who I thought he was.

Many things, I was learning, were not what they seemed. It appeared that it wasn't only me who was invisible. Everybody was invisible, since no one could see inside anybody else's head, and everybody used that invisibility to store up secrets, layer upon layer.

It wasn't far to Mr Maurice Bailey's house, but it was a slow walk. He was a rather overweight man, with a large belly that stuck out above his belt like a pregnant lady's. He moved at a leisurely pace, occasionally stopping to say hello to this or that person on the street. Mr Bailey seemed quite popular in Hedgecombe.

After about twenty minutes, we arrived at a tidy-looking detached house in a small cul-de-sac.

It had an imitation carriage lamp over the door and there was a gnome in the well-kept front garden, fishing and smoking a pipe. Parked on the drive was Mr Bailey's Land Rover, crouched there like a rusting hulk of history. Oil was dripping from underneath it onto the concrete below. He stopped to inspect it, stroking it with the tips of his fingers like he was in love with the thing. He stopped and wiped a blob of dirt from the wing, although the chassis was clogged with grime, so it seemed pointless.

Then Mr Bailey left his beloved Land Rover, opened his front door and took his shopping into the house. It wasn't difficult to follow him in since he left the door wide open. I wasn't sure whether he lived on his own or if he had a wife, but there weren't any obvious feminine touches like flowers or family photographs on the mantelpiece. His house was well-kept and nice, though – there was thick carpet and furniture with floral patterns on it. The surfaces all seemed polished and the windows clean. I liked it. There was a flag I didn't recognize on the wall – a white cross on a black background – and lots of pictures of English country scenes.

I decided to take a look upstairs while Mr Bailey unpacked his shopping. There were only two bedrooms. The first one I went into appeared to be Mr Bailey's – the wardrobe door was open and I could see his clothes hung up inside. Opposite the wardrobe was a single bed. The other bedroom, presumably the spare room, had twin beds, and a third room seemed to serve as an office.

I went into the third room. Here there was a desktop computer and a tray of papers and stationery. There was also a pile of leaflets, face down on the desk. I flipped them over. They featured a picture of a nice-looking, quite handsome family – three children and a mother and father. They were all smiling happily. The words printed in red across their chests read: "People Like You Voting WCDL".

Then I heard footsteps on the stairs. I pressed myself against the wall. Before I knew it, Mr Bailey had entered and closed the door firmly behind him. The room was very small. There was nowhere to hide. He was holding a cup of tea which he put down on the desk only centimetres away from where I was standing. I tried to keep my breathing as quiet as possible.

Mr Bailey sat down at his desk and switched on his

big, old-fashioned computer. As soon as the screen cleared, he went to his browser and typed in an address. A chatroom appeared on the screen.

I could see the screen quite clearly from where I stood. It appeared to be some kind of debate about how to "solve" the problem of mass immigration. The WCDL, it turned out, was the West Country Defence League. I assumed that Mr Bailey came from the west of England. The blog was headed with a large picture of the white-and-black flag I had seen downstairs, which I assumed now was some kind of West Country regional flag. I assumed the WCDL was some kind of offshoot of the English Defence League who had demonstrated in our part of London sometimes, not against black people, usually, but Muslims.

People were posting their suggestions. Most had put up more or less the same thing – that they had "nothing against" people of different races, but that their customs and traditions were different and that they should be allowed to develop separately from traditional British culture.

A few others said that "ethnic minorities" – so it wasn't just black people and Muslims – should be tolerated, but forced to learn English and adopt "English customs". I wondered what that meant – that they should be forced to eat crumpets and drink tea? And how did you force someone to learn the English language?

Then I found myself shivering – I hoped shivering didn't make a noise. Because Mr Bailey was now writing a comment himself. When I read what he had written, I had to blink twice to believe it.

Mr Bailey's post began: "Voluntary repatriation is not a complete solution."

Voluntary repatriation means that people who want to go back to the country that their family originally came from should be given the funds to do so by the government. So if your family is Jamaican, you could get money for returning to Jamaica. Or presumably, if you're Anglo Saxon, you could get money for returning to Saxony in Germany.

"Those who were not born here and are from a foreign, non-European culture," continued Mr Bailey, "should be sent back to their home countries – voluntarily ideally, forcibly if necessary."

This took a moment to sink in. I was deeply shocked and frightened. I had never met a real dyed-in-the-wool racist. I would never have dreamed they looked like Mr Bailey. I thought people like that were all skinheads and football hooligans. But Mr Bailey had always been pleasant to me, and he looked completely respectable.

I didn't like to think what Mr Bailey's reaction might be if he bumped into me, thus breaking whatever enchantment it was that kept me invisible, and revealing a thirteen-year-old, black, non-West Country child in his private sanctum. I doubted that it would involve him serving me Victoria sponge cake and lemonade.

I didn't manage to get out of that room for a terrifying half an hour, during which time Mr Bailey wrote horrible things on the forum about how "people from other countries and races" were "diluting our blood stock" and "destroying a proud, ancient race and a noble culture".

Then he went downstairs to make himself another cup of tea and watch *Countdown* like an ordinary person.

He had left the chatroom open. Now that he had gone, my fear was replaced with anger. I couldn't resist adding to Mr Bailey's comments in my own words.

Without sitting down, I did a quick Google search, and then I posted this:

"Everything I have written is rubbish. I have realized that I am a loony. I have just found out that 36,000 people of colour were killed fighting Hitler in the Second World War for Britain and that nearly three million wore a British uniform. I have decided that we owe these people and their descendants a great debt, and I am deeply ashamed of what I have written. Please don't take anything I write after this seriously. Now the nurse says it is time for my medication so I must say goodbye."

I snuck downstairs. Mr Bailey had made another cup of tea and got some biscuits and he was taking them outside. I followed him. He let himself into the house next door. I carried on following.

An old lady was sitting in the front room. She must have been a hundred. She seemed very pleased to see Mr Bailey, but barely able to talk. There were two crutches propped up against the wall. She was dribbling. He wiped the dribble away from her mouth, and then gently, slowly, fed her the tea and biscuits. He was still there, quietly feeding her, when I silently let myself out a few minutes later.

*

It was still only early afternoon. It was hotter than ever – weirdly so. I found my mobile phone and rang Susan Brown again. This time she answered. I suggested she might like to go swimming in the river – even though I couldn't swim. She agreed more readily than I expected and we set a time and place.

Within an hour, I had made myself visible again, collected my swimming trunks and a towel, and followed Susan's directions to a little spot on the River Hedge, maybe a mile outside the town centre. Susan met me by the roadside and then took me to her secret space. It was cut off from the rest of the riverbank, because you had to push through some heavy foliage to get there, but once you had made your way through, there was a bank overhung with willow trees. A little incline led down to the river where there was a small stretch of shore backed by head-height ferns, weeds and shrubs. It was like a hidden refuge. Sunlight pushed through a curtain of leaves and made the water seem a brilliant green, the colour of tree frogs.

We just sat there on the riverbank for a while, staring out at the water. I was still, I think, in a state of shock, both from finding out the truth about my father and also from discovering Mr Maurice Bailey's nasty secret. But somehow the water, the sunshine and the presence of Susan calmed and soothed me. I felt unexpectedly happy. I looked at Susan. The sunlight shining through the leaves was speckling on her cheeks.

"You look – yellowy-brown," I said. "Like you're made of gold."

She smiled, and looked happy, then sad, and muttered

something that I couldn't quite make out. When I said I couldn't hear her, she recited something:

"'Golden lads and girls all must,
As chimney-sweepers, come to dust.'"

When I looked puzzled, she said, "Shakespeare. I'm a literature nerd too."

Then, without warning and without embarrassment, she peeled off her clothes.

Underneath, she was wearing a two-piece swimming suit with a rose pattern on it. It wasn't sexy or anything. She just looked nice. But I noticed on her stomach a pale-red snaking scar. She saw me looking.

"I was ill once," she said. "But I'm all right now."

"How ill?" I said.

"Very," she said. "I nearly died, my mum and dad said. But the illness has gone away. Complete remission."

"That's good," I said, not knowing what else to say. I tried to cover up the awkwardness by going behind a tree and starting to get changed.

"It makes you grow up fast," she said, as I fumbled with my shoes and trunks and the towel.

"Does it?" I said, falling over as I stood on one foot to get my trouser leg off, then righting myself and finishing the job.

"It makes you realize you're just like any other person," she said. "Not that special at all."

It was then that I told her about my father – still standing behind the tree so I couldn't be seen. Susan listened without saying a word. When I'd finished, I peered around the tree. She had picked a leaf off the ground and was picking at it, peeling the epidermis slowly off the skeleton.

"I wonder why he would do that?" she said quietly.

I shook my head, unable to answer.

"I don't suppose he meant any harm," she continued. "Perhaps he just wanted you to look up to him. Perhaps he's insecure. Parents are people too, you know."

I finally emerged from behind the tree, slightly embarrassed but modestly attired, I hoped, in a large pair of swimming shorts tied with a cable at the waist.

"Well?" she said.

She clearly expected me to say something about my father, but I didn't know what to say. I supposed she was right, but I didn't really want to admit it.

"I disagree about what you said before," I said boldly.

She looked puzzled. "What did I say before?"

"You said you were not special. But I think you are very special."

I tried to hold her gaze, but hers was too steady. I looked away.

Then she whooped and laughed and I heard a splash. She was in the river, flicking me with water. The river by the bank was shallow. It only reached her waist, but she ducked down and covered herself with water, then bobbed up again.

"It's warm," she said. "Try it."

So I took a deep breath and jumped. The riverbed was muddy beneath my feet. The water was freezing. I screamed.

"It's BLOODY COLD!" I yelled.

She laughed even more.

"Like you always say – it's relative," she said, and ducked under again.

When she came up, I shivered and tried to take another step into deeper water, but she turned to me and shhhed me.

"Look," she said, pointing her finger.

I looked. Three swans were coming towards us in a perfect line. They were pure white and beautiful, and when they flapped their wings, a mist of water rose up and covered them, producing rainbows in the air. They stopped in front of us and seemed to be inspecting us. We stood still. They looked at us, and we looked at them.

Then they lost interest and moved on, majestically.

"It must be a sign," said Susan.

"Meaning what?" I said.

"Who knows?" she whispered back. And then she said, "Strato Nyman, I'm going to teach you to swim."

I said right away that I was scared to try and swim, but she said it was simple.

"All you have to do is trust the water," she said. "And then swimming is easy."

I did. She was right.

That afternoon, for the first time in my life, I swam six metres of simple breast stroke, in water that was too deep for me to stand up in. Susan guided me all the way. She held my hands, coaxed me through the green water, teased and cajoled me until I believed that swimming was no big thing. I felt safe around her, like nothing bad could happen.

Afterwards, as we stretched out on the riverbank, it seemed like we were the only two people in the world. No boats came past. No planes flew overhead. The world was absolutely still.

As the sun moved down in the sky, Susan reached for her bag and brought out two cheese-and-tomato sandwiches and a bottle of warm Coca-Cola. We ate and drank together, and I felt very happy.

We never touched. We never kissed. We didn't talk about my father again. All we discussed was science-geek stuff. Then we got dressed again and went straight home as if nothing special had really happened.

All the same, I knew it had been one of those afternoons I was going to remember for the rest of my life.

Because for those few hours, I no longer felt invisible. I felt I was *there* at last, and wanted to stay there. I was getting more filled in with colour, like crayons in the outline of a drawing, all the time.

CHAPTER THIRTEEN

WITCHES, ELOHIM AND DONALD DUCK

I said nothing to my father about having seen his office. I had still not made up my mind whether to challenge him on the matter or not. After discussing it with Susan, part of me felt sympathetic towards him, even though I didn't understand why he had felt the need to pretend he was still a big-shot scientist when he was now just a low-ranked paper shuffler. Maybe he was trying to protect Peaches. After all, it was her who had made us move down here.

Anyway, I didn't feel in the mood for a confrontation. Perhaps I would let him keep his little secret. After all, it wasn't only him who had something to hide, was it? Who was I to judge, when I was blatantly spying on him and Peaches?

Meanwhile, at school, Lloyd Archibald Turnbull's behaviour had improved. He had stopped bullying me and his attitude in class was markedly better. I suspected this was connected with my nocturnal visit to his mother. His relationship with Dr Ojebande had become reasonably civilized. But he was still capable of bad behaviour. I suppose old habits die hard.

Two weeks after my visit to the river, we had a physics lesson. It was particularly uninteresting – mostly Dr Ojebande giving us the atomic weights of elements to learn off by heart – and the whole class was restless and bored. Everyone was fidgeting, and Lloyd Turnbull was picking at the cuticles of the fingers of his bad hand. I knew that to be a bad sign.

Sure enough, while Dr Ojebande had his back turned and was writing on the board, a paper pellet hit Lloyd Turnbull in the face. I saw that Wayne Collingham, who was sitting two rows in front of him, facing Dr Ojebande, had flicked it. He grinned. Lloyd Turnbull looked back intently. It seemed that he took it as some kind of challenge.

I watched as Lloyd Turnbull rolled up a piece of chewing-gum wrapper into a ball and toyed with it idly, tossing it up and down in his palm. His eyes darted from side to side and, in a single movement, he flicked the ball at Wayne Collingham. But Collingham ducked just in time. It missed him entirely, and bounced off Dr Ojebande's head like a tiny ping-pong ball.

Dr Ojebande stopped writing immediately and froze in position at the blackboard.

Very slowly and deliberately, he turned to face the class. His green cat's eyes now seemed to contain tiny licks of red flame. He furiously scanned the room for the culprit. Eventually, his gaze came to rest on Lloyd Turnbull, who was trying to look innocent, although those in the class who had seen what had happened were shooting conspiratorial glances at him.

Lloyd Turnbull seemed to grow rather pale as Dr

Ojebande's eyes fell on him. I got the impression he regretted what he had just done, which perhaps he would not have done in the old days.

"Was that you, Turnbull?" said Dr Ojebande sharply.

"Was what me, Sir?" Lloyd Turnbull answered meekly.

"Someone threw a pellet at the back of my head."

"Why do you think it was me, Sir?"

"It always is you, Turnbull."

"No, Sir," said Lloyd Turnbull, his voice wavering unconvincingly. "I never did it."

Now Dr Ojebande's head swivelled to Wayne Collingham.

"Was it you, Collingham?"

"No, sir," said Collingham immediately.

"Was it Turnbull?"

Collingham hesitated. "Don't know, Sir."

"Fleet, did you flick something at me?"

"No, Sir."

"Then who did?"

Nobody spoke. Dr Ojebande began scanning the floor by the blackboard. He leaned over and picked something up. It was the pellet. He nodded to himself, as if he had just made an important discovery. Then he turned back to Lloyd Turnbull.

"I thought you were showing a marked improvement in your behaviour. I was just starting to have a little bit of faith in you, Turnbull. Just goes to show that a leopard can't change its spots."

"But, Sir…"

"Let me ask you again, Turnbull. Was it you who threw this wrapper?"

Lloyd Turnbull looked confused and a little bit panicky. It seemed important to him in a way it had never been before that Dr Ojebande thought he was innocent – even though he clearly wasn't. He shook his head mutely. Dr Ojebande unfolded the crumpled ball of paper and held it up for the class to see. It was a wrapper from a stick of Wrigley's Juicy Fruit chewing gum.

"Turn out your pockets, Turnbull."

Reluctantly, Lloyd Turnbull emptied out his pockets. A pack of Wrigley's Juicy Fruit chewing gum, with wrappers identical to the one flicked at the back of Dr Ojebande's head, appeared on the desk. Dr Ojebande picked up the pack between his thumb and finger and examined it.

"I would say this was fairly conclusive evidence. Good enough for me, in any case. So it is proven again. You are a vandal and a liar. Tonight you are going to have to stay after school again. I will call your mother and let her know that you are going to be late. From what I know of Mrs Turnbull, I don't think she'll be too pleased, but then you should have thought of that before you began misbehaving."

Lloyd Turnbull turned paler still. He looked like he had done when I'd seen him at home, just about ready to cry.

I put my hand up. Dr Ojebande's eye swivelled and fell on me.

"What is it, Nyman? Want to rub his face in it, do you, boy?"

"No, Sir," I said.

"What, then?" said Dr Ojebande. "Don't waste my time."

"It was me, sir."

"What was you? What are you talking about?"

"I flicked the pellet."

Dr Ojebande laughed out loud. Lloyd Turnbull turned and stared at me in amazement.

"You?" said Dr Ojebande. "Since when did you flick pellets? For that matter, I've never even seen you chew gum."

I felt in my pocket for the stick of gum Lloyd Turnbull had given me before the detention. I took it out and showed it to Dr Ojebande, who examined it, looking very puzzled.

Then he turned, faced me and snorted.

"You're pathetic, Nyman. Trying to be like the bad boys so you can fit in. I'd have thought you would have left all that behind you in the urban jungle from whence you came."

He paused, and picked up his Bible, as if he was considering something.

"I suppose at least you had the decency not to let someone else take the blame for your misbehaviour. That must count for something. Still, you must be punished for this. See me for an hour after school. Count yourself lucky I am not referring you to the head teacher."

Now he turned towards Lloyd Turnbull.

"Turnbull, I have no choice but to apologize. It's clear that you really have changed after all, and I have not done you justice. Please forgive me for jumping to conclusions. It was inappropriate and unprofessional."

Lloyd Turnbull said nothing, but just stared at me.

I looked away into the middle distance, careful not to make eye contact.

After class, in the playground, the two Waynes sidled up to me.

"Hey, Dark Matter. What's de matter?" said Wayne Fleet, in a faux-West Indian accent, while Wayne Collingham laughed and scratched his armpits.

The two Waynes weren't as clever as Lloyd Archibald Turnbull. They were old-school bullies, nasty and physical. One jostled me from one side and one from the other, pushing me with their shoulders.

"He's a black hole in space," said Wayne Collingham, giggling in a high-pitched tone.

They stopped suddenly when a single, big, powerful forearm appeared behind Wayne Fleet and brought his head sharply in contact with Wayne Collingham's.

It was the good arm of Lloyd Turnbull.

The two Waynes looked puzzled, then furious.

"What the eff is wrong with you, Bully?" said Wayne Fleet, rubbing the side of his head where it had hit Wayne Collingham.

He didn't really say "eff", but something far worse beginning with F. I don't like to write words like that down. They look ugly on the page, just as they sound ugly in the voice.

The two Waynes, incidentally, always called Lloyd Turnbull "Bully", a shortened version of his surname, as a kind of compliment.

"Leave him alone," said Lloyd Archibald Turnbull quietly, turning in my direction. "He's all right."

They stared at him. Wayne Fleet actually looked like

he was going to hit him, but then Lloyd Turnbull raised his super-muscled arm and made a fist, the blood vessels standing out like a weightlifter's, and Wayne Fleet's tensed body seemed to collapse slightly. He clearly was not prepared to risk getting into a fight with Lloyd Turnbull.

Spitting on the ground and cursing loudly, the two Waynes shuffled off back towards the school. Lloyd Turnbull looked at me blankly, as if he couldn't quite believe what he had just done. The school bell sounded for the end of break. I nodded, embarrassed, and wandered off in the direction of the school buildings. I was grateful to Lloyd Turnbull – but I really didn't know what to say to him. I just couldn't make up my mind whether he was my friend or my enemy. The evidence was too contradictory to form a reliable theory.

During my hour's detention with Dr Ojebande, he once again forbade me any distracting material. Instead, I sat and studied the top of Dr Ojebande's head as he buried his nose in a textbook. There was a patch of baldness on top, revealing a leathered, slightly freckly crown of mottled skin. I found this oddly touching for some reason.

For all my reservations about him, I thought Dr Ojebande was an intriguing character. He was unlike any of the other teachers at the school. He seemed to take his job, and his life, very seriously. I rarely saw him smile or talk to the other teachers. I couldn't imagine him as a young man, or with a wife, or on holiday in his swimming trunks. I thought he must always wear his dark suit and tie, even in bed.

After he dismissed me from the detention, I decided to

follow him to gather more information so I could formulate a more comprehensive theory about him. I darted into the boys' toilet, used the mirror, and emerged just in time to see Dr Ojebande leaving the school gates, his black Bible in one hand and a battered brown leather briefcase in the other.

He walked fast. He was hard to keep up with, and I was soon breathing heavily. The day was cold, so my breath was turning to vapour in the air, but it was so misty that I hoped no one would notice the little puffs of steam that were appearing out of nowhere as I made my way down the high street. The warm weather had disappeared without trace and Christmas decorations were already appearing in the shop windows.

At one point, I thought I had lost him, but then I glanced through the window of the SPAR supermarket and saw him in there, gazing at items on the confectionary shelves. I followed him in, being careful to avoid bumping into anyone. Fortunately, it wasn't very crowded.

I stood about a metre and a half away from him, watching. He had put his Bible in a shopping basket, and alongside it were the following: one packet of high-bran cereal, two 60-watt light bulbs, one small jar of Vaseline, three bread rolls, a tub of spreadable butter, an economy pack of bacon, a pair of nail clippers and a multipack of Curly Wurly chocolate bars. There was also a small value pack of Christmas cards with angels on the front of them.

This told me nothing surprising about Dr Ojebande, although I was taken aback that he was such a fan of Curly Wurly chocolate bars. They happened to be my favourite, and this made him seem more human somehow. I also wondered who he might send Christmas cards to. He seemed such a loner.

After leaving the supermarket, he headed off to the lanes in the centre of the town, carrying his Bible and his groceries in a plastic shopping bag. At no time did he acknowledge or speak to anyone else. Dr Ojebande always seemed to have an intense sense of purpose, as if he was on an urgent mission which no one could prevent him from fulfilling.

He was walking down one of the main alleyways when he swivelled on his heel and turned off to the right. The fog had risen and I almost lost him on several occasions, but I managed to track him down the passageway – which I now realized, with an eerie sense of foreboding, was the passageway that contained the bookshop where I had met the strange giant with the ginger moustache.

As before, the passageway was deserted. Bizarrely, the black bird with the white patch on its wing I had seen the first time I visited was still there, perched on the sign. Was it some kind of pet? I swear it looked at me, like an angry father looking at a petulant child.

Dr Ojebande disappeared into the half-lit shop, which was still stacked to the ceilings with mouldy old books. I felt very much that I wanted to follow him. Did he know the man with the ginger moustache? Or was it just a coincidence?

Unfortunately, I was unable to find out. When I tried the door of the shop, I found it to be locked. I peered through the dirty glass, but there was no sign of Dr Ojebande anywhere, or the man with the ginger moustache. I could hardly knock on the window, since I was invisible, and anyway, I didn't want Dr Ojebande to know I was following him. I had no choice but to wait. The bird stayed where it was, not moving or making a noise.

After I'd been standing in the freezing fog for fifteen minutes, Dr Ojebande finally emerged. He was carrying a large, leather-bound book with yellow pages under his arm. It looked very old. I got close enough to see the title, but little else.

It read, in big, Gothic, old-style type: "*The Discoverie of Witchcraft Volume XV* by Reginald Scot".

The dark was crowding in and the fog was getting thicker. Dr Ojebande kept marching at the same pace, though, and I rushed to keep up, although I didn't feel that I really wanted to. The whole thing was too unsettling.

After walking for ten minutes, Dr Ojebande cleared the outskirts of town where it falls away to the countryside. He made his way through a copse and over a trickling stream. His black shoes were caked with mud and the bottoms of his trousers were soaked, but he just kept walking.

Eventually, a building came into sight through the mist. As the outline became clear, I realized that it was an old church. It looked abandoned. A lot of the roof tiles were missing, and the churchyard, full of gravestones sticking out like teeth, was overgrown. None of the stones looked less than one hundred years old. The doors to the church were secured with a rusting chain and a large padlock, and the windows were boarded up.

I thought Dr Ojebande would certainly turn around

and go back, since he clearly wouldn't be able to get in. I had no idea what he was doing there in the first place.

But then he reached inside his jacket pocket and produced a key, with which he unlocked the padlock. The big old doors opened, and he went inside.

I stood out there among the gravestones in the fog and dark for several minutes, debating with myself whether to go in. By now I was frightened as well as cold and tired. The wood of the church door creaked, and the leaves blew about my feet like scuttling spiders.

I took a gulp of air and decided that as I had come this far, I might as well continue. Very carefully, I made my way through the open doors.

Inside, like in any church, there were pews and an aisle and an altar. It smelled of urine, tobacco and damp twigs. The stained-glass window above the altar was not boarded up like the rest. A few of the panes of glass were broken, but it was largely intact. It was not like a normal stained-glass window. Although there was a depiction of Christ, he was not dominant. There were primarily images of orbs and stars and planets, and what appeared to be mystical signs which I did not recognize. Above the top arch of the window, letters spelled out the word "Elohim".

Dr Ojebande was on his knees in front of the altar. He had taken out the book that he had got from the shop and appeared to be reading from it in a loud murmur. I inched closer to try and hear what he was saying. I could hear him breathing. His eyes were pressed closed. I couldn't make out his words, but finally, creeping forward very slowly, I got close enough to see the page from which he was reading. This is what it said:

I call upon thee, I beseech thee O Lord Jesus Christ,
by the merits of thy blessed mother S. Marie, and of all
thy saints, that thou give me grace and divine power
over all the wicked spirits, so as they may come by
and by from everie coast, and accomplish my will, that
they neither be hurtfull or fearefull unto me,
but rather obedient—

And at that point my mobile phone went off.

I have different ringtones for when different people call me. The tone for my father is a strumming guitar. The tone for Susan is a string quartet playing.

The tone for my mother is Donald Duck.

The sound of a cartoon duck quacking echoed around the interior of the church.

Dr Ojebande's head whipped around. His green eyes were wide and startled. He looked frightened – then angry.

He held his Bible up in the air, closed his eyes and started to speak in loud, sonorous tones: *"Per crucis hoc signum fugiat procul omne malignum; Et per idem signum salvetur quodque benignum…"*

I didn't have a clue what he was talking about, and I wasn't going to hang around to find out. I turned and ran as fast as I could.

Was I still invisible? I wasn't sure. Dr Ojebande knew something was amiss – but perhaps he did not know that I was invisible, and so maybe the magic was preserved. I would not know until I found a mirror.

*

I ran all the way back to town, until I saw a sign for a public toilet. I rushed in, and on the wall was what was almost a mirror. It was, in fact, a piece of polished metal that was meant to be used as a mirror, but was unbreakable. It was scratched and warped, but I could see that I was not reflected in it. I breathed a sigh of relief. Dr Ojebande had not guessed where the ringing had come from. He did not know that I was invisible.

I felt the urgent need to be visible again. Oddly enough, it felt safer. I checked the polished metal again. Did it qualify as a mirror? I wasn't sure, but I was desperate enough to give it a go. I took my book, held it to my chest and ran full pelt at the sheet of steel.

I whacked into it with a thud, bounced off and slammed to the ground. My head reeled, and my nose was bleeding. It felt like I had sprained my wrist.

Clearly, the book did not consider the sheet of metal to be a proper mirror.

I ran out of the toilets and made my way to a nearby pub. The toilets there had a real mirror, and a few seconds later I was visible again. My face was a mess – bruised and covered with blood.

I cleaned myself up as best I could, then started limping towards home, my wrist aching, holding a tissue to my streaming nose. Then I decided to check my phone. My mother had left a message.

She sounded very upset.

"You need to come home, Strato. Something bad has happened. We need to talk."

It looked like my day wasn't about to get any better.

CHAPTER FOURTEEN

A CHOCOLATE ON THE PILLOW AT THE HEDGECOMBE TRAVELODGE

When I got home, Peaches was standing by the door, waiting for me. She looked stern and angry.

"He's gone, Strato."

"Who's gone?"

"Your father. He's moved out."

So it had happened at last. I felt I was going to be sick, and I reeled away from her. She saw my face.

"What happened to you? You look like you've been in a fight."

"It doesn't matter what happened to me! Where is he?"

I wiped the blood from my nose and fought back the tears from my eyes. My mother grabbed a tissue from the box on the telephone table and dabbed at my face ineffectually.

"He's in a hotel, just a mile away. But listen—"

"Give me the address."

"Strato. Wait. Let's talk. You and I."

"Give me the address. I want to see my father. I have something I need to ask him."

"Come and have some tea first. You look sick and starved, and it's cold and dark out there. I'll make you some hot chocolate with marshmallows. I'll do some cheese on toast. Or there's some jambalaya on the stove. And rice pudding for dessert."

Jambalaya was one of her specialities from the old country – basically spicy chicken, beans and rice. I liked it, but I wasn't in the mood.

"Peaches," I said. "It's all right. I'll be back very soon. I'm OK. But I need to see Melchior. I have a right to see my father, don't I?"

She nodded and shrugged. "I suppose…"

Her mouth was tight and fierce. It was as if the argument she had just had with Melchior was still taking place inside her head.

"He's done a bad thing, Strato. Some might say an unforgivable thing."

"Don't say bad things about Melchior. Just give me the address, Mother. *Please.*"

She stared at me, then grabbed a scrap of paper and a pencil and scribbled an address. She watched, dry-eyed, as I made my way off into the night.

I wanted to see my father straight away. I wanted to work out how to put this all to rights. After all, what was the point of having a special power if I couldn't use it to make things better?

Susan Brown's house was on the way, and I wondered briefly if I should stop in and talk to her about what my next step might be. But I wanted to see Melchior too urgently.

I arrived at the address Peaches had given me. A sign outside said "Hedgecombe Travelodge". It didn't look like a hotel – it looked like a row of red-brick Barratt houses in an industrial suburb.

Melchior was still unloading some of his things from the car. He was wearing a cardigan with a hole in one elbow. He smiled thinly when he saw me, then touched me on my nose exactly where I'd cut myself running into the mirror. I flinched.

"How did you do that?" he asked.

"I walked into a glass door," I said. (It was almost true.)

He nodded slightly and then, very unusually for him, he gave me a brief, but very tight, hug.

He stared at me with an unreadable expression on his face. I suggested politely that we went inside and sat down, as if I was the adult and he was the child, and he followed my instructions.

The room he was staying in was small, dark and sparsely furnished. I sat down on a plain wooden chair, and he sat on the bed. We remained there in silence for a while. A question was pressing at the edges of my mouth. I tried to keep it inside, but it was so strong that it burst out: "Why did you leave?"

"It wasn't me, Strato. I didn't want to go. Your mother told me I should."

I thought back to what Peaches had said. She hadn't explicitly claimed that Melchior had left of his own accord, but it had certainly been implied.

"Why? Why would she do that?"

This question left Melchior squirming uncomfortably on the bed.

"Your mother found a letter. From … this lady who I…"

"The lady you were having sex with."

Melchior looked startled, then stared down at the floor. "How did you know about her?"

"Because I'm not blind and deaf."

"What do you know?" he said in a very quiet voice.

"I know that you had a 'fling'. I know that her name was Annabel. I know Peaches made you move down here to get away from her. I know she made you give up your job. I know you didn't want to come, for my sake."

"What has Peaches been saying to you?" Melchior asked.

"I overheard some of your conversations."

"You've been snooping!"

"You're not really in any position to judge me, are you, Father?" I said quietly.

Melchior conceded the point. Then he sighed, and said, "Somehow she – Annabel – found out my address in Hedgecombe. She sent me a letter asking me to go back to London to see her. I didn't answer it. I put the letter at the bottom of the dustbin. I should have burned it. Peaches – she has a suspicious mind. She checked the rubbish. Apparently she does this regularly. She found the letter. And now she thinks we've been 'in touch'. But we haven't. This … this lady in London. She means nothing to me. I was going through a bad time. I was flattered that she liked me. I just made a mistake. Anyone can make a mistake. But your mother thinks that I was in love with her. That I am still in love with her. So after she found the letter – she threw me out. And here I am."

Now he looked at me pleadingly, begging with

his eyes for me to forgive him.

"You don't love this lady, then?" I asked. "This … Annabel?"

"Of course not! She's just a kid. A trainee. She was—"

"I don't want to know any more details."

"Oh. OK."

"I just want to ask you another question."

Melchior looked puzzled. "What's that, then?"

"It's this – why should I believe a single bloody word you say?"

"What?"

"You're a liar."

Melchior looked around the room as if he was searching for something. But whatever it was, it didn't appear to be there.

"I'm not a liar. Why are you saying that?" he said at last.

"Can I ask you another question?"

Melchior stood up and began to pace around the tiny room. Two of his suitcases were on the floor. There was a single chocolate on the pillow, wrapped in golden foil. Somehow the chocolate seemed particularly full of pathos.

"Pathos", incidentally, means "a quality that arouses pity".

"Anything, Strato. It's important that you know the truth. You're old enough. We need to be honest. Honesty is important."

"I agree. So … why did you pretend that you had a job down here working in a laboratory, when all you do is push paper in an office?"

Melchior almost toppled backwards. No doubt he

had been expecting a question about himself and my mother. This had taken him entirely by surprise.

"What are you talking about?" he said. But his heart wasn't in it.

"Don't make it worse," I said.

The muscles in his face seemed to tighten, then they relaxed into a forlorn expression.

"But – how did you know? Did Peaches tell you?"

"No, she didn't. It doesn't matter how I know. But I don't understand how you could give up your job as a scientist in the laboratory in London to come here and work in a desk job. Nothing could be worth that. Could it?"

Now Melchior looked even more despairing. He hesitated, then said, "No. I suppose not. Except that…"

He seemed to be engaged in a titanic struggle with himself.

"Tell me the truth, Melchior."

Melchior nodded. "OK. I'll tell you the truth."

He picked up the foil-wrapped chocolate and began picking at it with his fingernails.

He looked up at me. There were tears in his eyes. Water and salt and a few trace elements.

"I wanted to inspire you, Strato. I wanted you to respect me. Because you are so clever, and I am so ordinary. That makes me feel bad. It makes me feel stupid. So I pretended that I was more special than I actually am. Yes, I gave up the job in London to come down here. Yes, it had something to do with Peaches. But they were going to get rid of me at the lab anyway. I wasn't sharp enough any more. I couldn't cut the mustard. They offered me redundancy and I took it. If I hadn't, they would have sacked me."

I was having acute difficulty taking this on board. I felt myself blinking again and again, as if I had something stuck in my eye.

Then my father put his hand over mine and looked me directly in the eyes.

"I'm a foolish man, I know. But I'm not a bad man."

"You're a bad cook."

He smiled weakly.

"Yes, I'm a bad cook. But whatever I am, I love you, and I love your mother. All the way to the stars and back."

That was something he used to say when I was a small boy. He hadn't used that phrase for a very long time.

He picked the rest of the foil off the chocolate, leaving a trail of gold paper on the carpet.

"Can you forgive me, Strato?"

He put the chocolate untasted on the bedside table. It had the Travelodge logo imprinted on it.

I thought for a second, then I picked up the chocolate and swallowed it. I looked straight back at Melchior.

"What are you talking about, Father?"

He looked at his feet. "I suppose it's too much to expect."

I went and stood by Melchior. "I don't care *what* you do for a living. I don't care if you're a clerk or a particle physicist. You're my father. You don't need to hide things from me. I don't *care*. I love you, Dad. If you were a dustman, or an estate agent, or an unsuccessful rat catcher, I would love you the same."

Melchior didn't move for a moment – and then he

hugged me so hard I thought my bones would break. I wanted to cry, but I hardly ever cry, so I didn't.

After a while, we broke apart. Then Melchior made us both a cup of tea from the automatic tea-and-coffee-maker on the bedside table, and we sat and chatted for another hour.

He told me everything – about the woman in London, how it had only been a brief fling, how he was terrible at lying so Peaches found out right away and insisted they move away to the country. And that now they were in Hedgecombe, nothing had got any better, and he had to move out of the house.

"I keep thinking that if I could just say the right thing, Strato, she would take me back, and everything would be OK again. I still love her very much. And I believe that she still loves me too. I made a terrible mistake. But I don't know what the right thing to do is. I just don't know."

"Don't worry, Dad. I'll find out what the right thing to do is. Then everything will be OK again."

"How can you know that, Fender? You're thirteen years old. There's so much you don't understand."

I don't know why, but I really did believe that everything would be OK. I didn't have any evidence, but I believed it, absolutely. Peaches would doubtless have called it faith. Faith is an entirely unscientific concept. But on this occasion it felt entirely tangible.

When I got home, Peaches was nowhere to be seen. I assumed that she was in her study. She was very strict about her work hours. I suspected that even the trauma of the past few hours was insufficient to stop her in her tracks. The dinner that she'd made me was on the table, but it had gone cold. I put it in the microwave, and munched my way through it.

As I was eating the last of my rice pudding, also reheated in the microwave, I looked at the wall calendar. There was an appointment, scrawled in Peaches' handwriting. Tomorrow, Dorothea Beckwith-Hinds was coming to stay overnight. There was certainly only going to be one topic of conversation. My mother and her friends loved to talk about relationships, and they would certainly have plenty to talk about now.

Peaches didn't like to be disturbed when she was writing. But, given the circumstances, I felt I was justified in interrupting her. I opened her door without knocking. She continued to stare at her computer screen as I walked in.

"Are you OK, dahlin'?"

"Given that my father has just moved out of the house, I thought you might want to engage with me for a minute or two."

My mother sighed.

"I do. Of course I do. I'm sorry, Strato. Sometimes I just get so – distracted. Writing the book, I mean."

She rose from her chair and put her arm around me.

"Welcome to the Geek Farm, you mean?"

Peaches took her arm away from her shoulders.

"Did Melchior tell you? That rotten son of a…!"

"No. I found out on my own. And don't call him a rotten anything. He's not."

She nodded, but it was pretty obvious that she didn't agree with me.

I ignored this.

"I understand that the book concerns me," I continued. "I'm the geek, right?"

Now she had the decency to blush.

"Well – not just you—"

She broke off, apparently realizing that this wasn't a very effective line of defence.

"Look, Strato. I don't expect you to understand. But I've got a publisher interested in this book. In fact, more than interested – they definitely want to publish it. It will be the start of a whole new career for me. We will be able to look after ourselves, Strato. Even if your father and I end up…"

Her voice tailed off.

"Splitting up for good?" I said.

She nodded.

"What about me?"

"I know it's hard for you, Strato. But lots of children have parents who—"

This time I interrupted.

"I'm not talking about you and Melchior. Do you think it's OK to write a book about me without asking my permission?"

Peaches looked shocked.

"I *was* going to ask your permission, Strato. In due course. Of course I was."

"Of course. Well, why wait? Ask me now."

"Now?"

"Yes – now."

My mother took a sip of water from a glass on her desk and looked me up and down.

"I'm not sure this is the right time and place."

"It is for me."

"But you don't know what it's about."

"It's about me and you and the difficulties of bringing up a gifted and talented child."

"Well, yes … but until you read it…"

"I don't need to read it. Just ask me if it's OK to write it."

I could tell that she couldn't quite decide what to do. Then she gave a small nod, as if she had made a private decision, and turned to me.

"Strato. My little genius gorgeous boy. Do I have your permission to write this book?"

"What if I say no?"

She paused again. "If you say no, then I won't write it."

"Good. Then the answer is no."

I walked out of her room, leaving her with her mouth hanging open about two centimetres, with her tongue protruding slightly like a little animal trying to escape.

CHAPTER FIFTEEN

THINGS THAT ARE VERY MUCH NOT OK

The next day on the bus to school, I found Susan Brown saving a seat for me. I sat down, but I didn't quite know what to say. I felt something special had happened that afternoon down by the river, but it embarrassed me to think about it. So I took refuge in a familiar subject – science.

I told her I had a genius theory about gravity and light – that they are really the same thing. No other scientist in the world believed this, but I did, because I couldn't see any other possible explanation.

She nodded and looked genuinely interested, which only about one in a million girls of her age would do.

"Albert Einstein came up with this super-good thought experiment. He asked himself a very simple question. (He was good at very simple questions.) He asked himself, 'What if the Sun were suddenly to disappear? What would happen to the Earth?'"

Susan looked at me with an interrogative expression on her face.

"Interrogative", incidentally, means "questioning".

187

"Obviously, it would get very dark and very cold very quickly and then we would all die. What's the big puzzle there?" said Susan.

"Yes, but something else would happen very quickly. The Earth would fly off its orbit, because it no longer had the Sun to keep it in place. It would spin out into deep space until it found another big object to attach itself to."

Susan nodded. "So what?"

"The question is, which would happen first? Which is to say, what travels faster – gravity or light?"

"Does gravity travel?"

"It must do – somehow. It sticks the whole universe together."

"So which one *does* happen first?"

"That's the interesting thing. Einstein concluded that they travel at exactly the same rate – 300,000 kilometres per second. And pretty much every scientist nowadays agrees with him."

"So your theory is…?"

"It's simple. If these two giant super-weird forces in the universe travel at *exactly* the same speed – it must mean that they are really the same thing! Otherwise it's just too much of a coincidence."

Susan laughed. "So you're the only one who's actually worked this out, are you?"

"I admit, it does sound improbable. But my father says sometimes scientists can't see the wood for the trees. Which is why Einstein was so brilliant – because he saw what was *so* simple. No one else could understand it."

On the way off the bus, Mr Maurice Bailey grinned,

and called, "Goodbye, Robertson," after me. I turned and glared at him. He didn't seem to notice – he just carried on grinning.

As we were walking into school, I asked Susan why he was calling me Robertson.

She paused, and then she told me that there was a company called Robertson's which used to put a golliwog – which is a crude stereotypical representation of a black minstrel, with frizzy hair and bulging eyes – on the jars of its marmalade, until people pointed out that this was racially prejudiced. They stopped doing it, but a lot of people who liked Robertson's marmalade believed that they shouldn't have stopped, because it was part of "British culture".

I rather suspected that one of those people was Mr Maurice Bailey.

"We've got to get him, Strato – somehow," said Susan.

I agreed. But I wasn't sure how to do it.

Susan headed off to the library and I found myself standing alone in the playground. I felt a tap on my shoulder. I turned. It was Lloyd Archibald Turnbull.

He was holding something in his good hand. There was a moment's silence before he spoke. It was almost as if he was plucking up the courage. Then he said, "I brought something for you."

He handed me a copy of the second volume of George R. R. Martin's *A Song of Ice and Fire* series: *A Clash of Kings*.

"It's better than the first one. I've read them all. You can keep this. And I can lend you the rest. Let me know what you think of it."

He set off towards the classroom whistling, leaving me staring at the book in astonishment.

That evening, Peaches' best friend, Dorothea, arrived. I had never much liked Dorothea. She always struck me as enjoying other people's troubles too much. In London, I'd often heard her and my mother picking over the smallest details of people's relationships, to see where the cracks were. They positively enjoyed it, I think, although they always used to say how sorry they were for the couple having difficulties.

That's another difference between children and adults. Children bully one another, but they are not usually nasty while pretending that they are being nice. Obviously, Lloyd Archibald Turnbull was a bully, or at least he had been. But he knew he was being nasty. He just didn't care. Dorothea probably thought she was being perfectly nice. She would often begin her attacks with a compliment. She would say something like, "I really admire X or Y for trying to lose weight – but it's a bit of a lost cause, isn't it? Like trying to climb the Matterhorn in a pair of high heels. Or getting a walrus to do push-ups."

Dorothea was going to have a field day. Her very best friend, Peaches, was on the point of breaking up with her partner, my father, for good.

She came dressed in smart London clothes and had thick make-up plastered on her face. I heard her tell Peaches that she had spent £500 on her handbag, and that it was worth every penny, which struck me as hilariously stupid.

Although she made sympathetic faces about our

family "situation" – at me as well as Peaches – I could tell all her Christmases had come at once. She couldn't wait to sit down and talk through all the intimate details over a bottle of wine. Peaches immediately sent me upstairs and closed the door.

I went upstairs obediently, but when I came down again, I was nowhere to be seen. I peeked through a crack in the door, and when they were both looking the other way, I crept into the kitchen to join them and closed the door behind me.

What followed was one of the least interesting experiences of my life.

For a start, I'm male, and males find different things interesting to females. Also, I was a child – just about – and children find different things interesting to adults. But quite apart from these considerations, sitting and listening to Dorothea and Peaches pick through the minutiae of not only their own relationships, but, it seemed, every mutual friend's, was more than anyone could bear.

It was a good two hours before they actually got around to talking about Peaches and Melchior, because it seemed that Dorothea herself was having problems with her marriage. Apparently she preferred to tell Peaches at great length about Simon (her husband) and how he didn't appreciate her, and how he never listened to her, and how he failed to see her true potential as a human being, and how he was uncommunicative and withdrawn and so on.

I was only thirteen, but from my experience these appeared to be simply the standard complaints that wives made about their husbands – if Peaches' and Melchior's relationship was anything to go by. However, Dorothea seemed to think that she was the first person ever to experience these difficulties, and Peaches seemed to go along with the show, nodding sympathetically and interjecting "supportive" comments.

However, they finally got on to Melchior and Peaches, and for another hour, I was treated to a lot more twaddle – about how they needed to "get back in touch" with their feelings, how Peaches needed to "reconnect with her centre", how Melchior was "insensitive to her needs", and so on and so forth.

I had been hoping to find some clue as to how I might get them back together, but all I heard was self-pity. Being scientifically minded, I like to hear practical suggestions – but none whatsoever was forthcoming.

It was at least clear from the conversation that Peaches still loved Melchior, but that she found his fling in London unforgivable, however hard she tried to get beyond it, and that although he'd tried to compensate by leaving London, the letter in the bin had been the final straw. Finally, Dorothea asked the 64-million-dollar question – was there anything that Melchior could do to get Peaches to take him back?

Peaches hummed and hawed about the answer, and made noises about doubting whether they could ever get over what had happened to them, but then she said one thing that gave me hope.

"What I need from Melchior," said Peaches, "is a really big gesture. One that shows me how much he cares. One that shows me he is truly sorry. That it's not just words."

"What might that gesture look like?" said Dorothea,

looking past Peaches' shoulder and out of the window. It had been clear for some time that, having offloaded her own troubles, she was bored with sifting through Peaches'.

"I don't know," said Peaches. Then again, this time in a kind of a despairing voice, "I don't know."

They drained their wine glasses and finished the conversation by giving each other a hug.

Then they got on to the subject of "the book". Dorothea's company, of course, was going to publish it.

"Everyone is terribly excited about it, Marie-France," said Dorothea. "They think they've got a real hot property. They're going to spend a lot of money promoting it. How's it going? Are you nearly finished yet?"

"Yes," said Peaches. "I'm just doing a final edit."

"That's wonderful!" said Dorothea, pouring herself another glass of wine. "You must let me see it. I'm dying to read it. Is it good? Are you pleased with it?"

"I think the publishers will like it," said Peaches glumly.

Dorothea pursed her lips and looked at Peaches enquiringly. "What on earth is the matter, Marie-France? You look positively forlorn. Is it end-of-book blues? I've heard a lot of authors say that they get very down-in-the-mouth at the end of a long project."

"It's not that, no."

Then she told Dorothea that I had found out about it and wasn't very happy.

Dorothea clucked and waved her hand airily in the direction of my bedroom.

"Oh, he's being ridiculous. He'll get over it. After all, you've only been honest, haven't you? What's there to hurt him?"

"I've given it some thought, which is something I should have done a long time ago, and there's quite a lot that he might not like, actually."

"Yes, but – this is your big opportunity, Marie-France! It may never come again."

"I wish I'd talked to Strato about it first. Melchior said I should have."

"Melchior! What does he know? And Strato's simply too young to make that judgement for himself. He'll thank you when he's being driven around in a brand-new BMW bought with the money you've made from the book."

"I'm not so sure."

"Of course he will. Children have very short memories. Anyway, none of his friends will read it."

"Bits of it could easily end up on Facebook. He hasn't got many friends, as far as I'm aware. My book isn't going to help matters. Anyway…" She hesitated. "I asked his permission to publish it."

Dorothea put down her wine and regarded Peaches steadily. "And what did he say?"

"He said no."

Dorothea shuffled in her seat and adjusted the collar of her shirt as if she was making sure her point of view was still neatly in place.

"Now listen, Marie-France. You'd better not be going cold on this thing. Because apart from anything else, it's my reputation on the line as well as yours. You've been paid a considerable advance for this book. Are you prepared to pay it back?"

"I can't. I've spent it."

"Quite. Well, be under no illusions. If you don't give

them the book, you'll have to pay the money back."

Peaches by now was looking quite bereft. "Perhaps I could just change the title?"

"Absolutely not! I sold it on the title. It's a great title. It's what's going to make people buy the book."

"But – it's saying that Strato is a geek!"

"Let's face it, dear. He's a bit on the spectrum, isn't he?"

I think Dorothea was referring to the autism spectrum. Autistic people have a great deal of difficulty showing or experiencing emotion or empathy. They are often obsessed with orderliness and sometimes exhibit obsessive-compulsive behaviour.

If I hadn't been so clear in my own mind that I was nowhere whatsoever on that particular spectrum, I would have been offended. But she was so far off the mark, I didn't let it get to me too badly. If she thought I was obsessed by orderliness she ought to take a look at my room sometime. However, I was still annoyed at her blunt and insensitive attempt to stereotype me as someone who suffered some kind of mental impairment.

"Now tell me, Marie-France. Tell me right to my face. You're going to finish this book, aren't you? And you're going to deliver it into my hands before Christmas. And it's going to be a big success, and your career is going to take off in a way you could never have imagined."

Peaches looked at Dorothea with a doubtful expression on her face. "Is it?"

Dorothea took Peaches' left hand between her own, and squeezed it.

"It is. Your life will never be the same."

*

A few days later, I went round to Susan Brown's house. As before, her family were overwhelming in their hospitality and we had supper together – something with Italian sausages and rocket salad – and then Susan and I went to her room to watch a DVD of *Mr Bean*, which made us both laugh till we almost urinated.

I had decided something before I went into Susan's room – that I wanted to kiss her.

I knew I was only thirteen, but I couldn't deny the feelings I was having towards her. She was so pretty and so nice, I couldn't help it. She gave me a feeling in the pit of my stomach which I couldn't understand, but it was a very good feeling and it made me want to touch her and stroke her hair.

The only thing was, I didn't understand anything about girls at all, or kissing. I wasn't sure whether I should just reach over and kiss her without saying anything, like they did in some films I'd seen, or whether I should work my way up to it somehow. Perhaps I should bring her roses or poems or something, or maybe I should discuss the matter rationally with her.

I decided the best course of action was the latter. It was certainly the one I felt most comfortable with – after all, I didn't want to be accused of taking advantage of her, or pressing her with my unwanted attentions.

So once the film was finished and we'd finished the popcorn and hot chocolate that Mrs Brown had brought up to us, I decided to outline my difficulty. I tried to look at her face, but for some reason I found it very difficult to do, so I looked at the floor instead. This probably wasn't a good tactic, but it was all I felt capable of.

Then I said to her, "Susan, can I talk to you about something?"

She said I could.

Then I said, "Susan, I think you are very pretty."

She smiled but didn't say anything.

Then I said, "I like being with you. I think you are fun and clever."

Still she didn't say anything. Sometimes in films when this happens and the boy doesn't know what to do next, the girl reaches over and kisses him, so he doesn't have to worry about it any more. But on this occasion nothing like that seemed to be happening. Susan just smiled. I got the impression she was very close to giggling.

Then there was a very awkward silence in which I didn't really get up the courage to ask her if I could kiss her. Asking if I could kiss her felt wrong, too formal or something, but then just reaching across and trying to kiss her felt too rude.

At that moment, Mrs Brown walked in with a plate of biscuits and sat down with us, so the moment passed. On one hand, I was enormously relieved by this, and on the other, considerably disappointed.

My disappointment didn't last, because Mrs Brown was such fun. She told us jokes, and teased me for being so handsome, which was ridiculous, but still nice to hear. I felt so comfortable with her. And before I knew it, I found that I was telling her all about Melchior's and Peaches' problems, and the conversation I had "overheard accidentally" between Dorothea and Peaches, and that I wished I could think of a "Big Gesture" for my father to make so that he and Peaches could get back together.

That started it. Susan and Mrs Brown began going through all the things that Melchior could do to win Peaches back. A string quartet on the front lawn. A room full of flowers. A brand-new Mini. A balloon ride across the mountains. A horse of her own. Their ideas were endless, and clever, and quite good.

But something told me that none of them was quite good enough. I was no closer to knowing what the Big Gesture should be, and even if I could think of it, how would I get Melchior to listen?

CHAPTER SIXTEEN

THE HOUSE OF THE *DYN HYSBYS*

Now that I was friends with Susan, school was much more bearable, and time seemed to pass much more quickly. Before I knew it, Christmas was closing in.

There were decorations, cards and illuminated Christmas trees in the windows of the houses, and some had neon-lit reindeer outside. There had been a snow-fall a few days previously, and the streets and roofs still glittered white. Hedgecombe was made for Christmas with its winding lanes, ancient houses and rolling hills in the background. It felt very seasonal, and if it hadn't been for my parents splitting up, I'm sure I would have been very excited instead of being filled with dread and foreboding.

It was on the last day of term that I decided to follow Dr Ojebande for a second time. My previous attempt to trail him had left me full of questions. Why had he bought a book on witchcraft? Was he in cahoots with the man who had sold me my book? What had he been visiting a disused church for, and why did he have the key? Who was he? Did he have friends or relatives? What sort of home did he have? I had no clear intention of using my power to solve a particular problem. I was just curious, plain and simple. He was an excellent subject for my observation experiment. I just wasn't sure how to create a theory around him.

School finished early that day, and I waited outside the school gates for him, invisibly. He arrived after nearly everyone else had left, at exactly 3.30 p.m., marching briskly, as before. This time he did not go to the shops, but immediately headed out of town, in the opposite direction to where the old disused church had been.

It was a cold afternoon, and as it did so often in Hedgecombe, fog had rolled into the town from the rivers and lowlands. I followed Dr Ojebande as best I could, peering through the dank, misty air. It was all I could do to keep up. He walked through the west side of the town until the buildings thinned out, and along a muddy track on the bank of the river, until the buildings ended altogether. There were only fields, trees and fences, all swathed in white. The mist kept rising, and the feeble sun had slunk permanently behind an immense bank of purple-black cloud like a vast celestial bruise.

After another fifteen minutes' quick marching – by now it was beginning to rain, converting snow into muddy sludge – he left the track, jumped a fence and started walking across a rutted field, in the corner of which there was an enormous, stocky-looking bull. The bull raised its head and began slowly pacing towards him.

Then some kind of huge, black bird – a crow? A raven? – flapped down from a nearby tree, and came to perch on his shoulder. I noticed that it had a white mark on its wing, roughly in the shape of a figure eight. It was my old friend from the bookshop. What on earth was it doing there?

Instead of shrieking and trying to dislodge the bird, as anyone else might have done, he took no notice of it. With the bird perched on his shoulder – it was almost as big as his head – he kept on striding towards a curtain of silver birch trees, pale and ghostly, on the far side of the field.

This spectacle was undoubtedly Gothic, but I didn't have too much time to think about it because, to my alarm, the bull started to trot, then actually charge, in our direction.

"Gothic", incidentally, is a movement of the nineteenth century which encompassed horror stories and ghost stories: for example, the work of Edgar Allan Poe and Mary Shelley, who wrote *Frankenstein*.

The bull's head was at the height of my shoulders, and its horns curved forwards, each ending in a sharp-looking point. It increased its pace. It was now maybe fifteen metres away. I somehow suppressed the urge to bolt and hoped it was coming for Dr Ojebande rather than me.

When the bull was maybe ten metres away and I had decided that Dr Ojebande was definitely going to get flipped and probably gored to death, Dr Ojebande calmly turned and stared pointedly at the bull, before continuing through the field. To my amazement, at that exact moment, the bull stopped dead. It didn't retreat or change direction. It just stopped, and didn't move again until Dr Ojebande had left the field.

The crow – or whatever it was – had flown from

Dr Ojebande's shoulder, and Dr Ojebande was climbing over another fence, making his way through a gap in the row of silver birch trees. I clambered over the fence as quietly as I could. It was topped with barbed wire – my trousers got caught and tore. It took me nearly a minute to free them. By the time I had done so and had burst through the silver birch trees, Dr Ojebande was nowhere to be seen.

The fog was getting thicker and soon I could see practically nothing. I considered giving up and going home, but that would have meant going through the field with the bull in it again and I wasn't sure that it was going to remain quite so accommodating without Dr Ojebande there to stop it.

I decided to keep walking in the direction I thought Dr Ojebande had been heading in, but with each step I felt more and more nervous. I feared I was getting well and truly lost. I had no idea where I was, and now there were trees on every side. The rain was getting heavier, the light was fading and the fog was as impenetrable as soggy cotton wool. I just felt like sitting down and crying, but it was too cold and I had come too far. Besides, as I've said, I never cry.

Just then I saw a shape rising out of the mist. An old grey cottage with a thatched roof in need of repair, and an overgrown, untidy garden. A chimney plumed smoke into the air and a very faint light gleamed in the windows.

This had to be Dr Ojebande's house. As I got closer, though, it seemed to bear very few signs of habitation. There was no noise coming from within.

Then the oddest sound cut through the silence.

It wasn't a human voice – more like something my electric voice changer would have come up with. It spoke what I recognized as one word, again and again: "Beware. Beware. Beware."

It was the black bird again. Was it really saying "beware"? I wasn't sure of anything right at that moment.

The front door opened and Dr Ojebande, still in his black suit, emerged. There was a pile of logs to the right of the door, and he picked up an armful, presumably to throw on the fire.

If I was going to get into his house at all – although I wasn't sure that I wanted to – this was my chance. It was now or never, so when he bent down to pick up another log, I silently darted inside.

What met my eyes – as Dr Ojebande followed me, shutting the door behind both of us – did nothing to reduce my anxiety.

Instead of a carpet, the room had a bare stone floor. The roof was low and beamed. It was dark in there, and it smelled strange, like cloves and rotten apples. There were no electric lights on, only a number of candles lit around the room. The only other light came from a large stone fireplace. Dr Ojebande knelt down and carefully placed the logs on the flames.

On the walls were mounted stuffed animal heads – a bear, a deer, and something with horns that I didn't recognize. There were three chairs, each of them hard and upright, carved with strange figures and symbols. There were books, but they were very old and musty-looking, like the ones I had seen in the bookshop where the man with the ginger moustache had given me *How To Be Invisible*.

I turned and saw Dr Ojebande standing beside an old-fashioned gramophone. At first I heard the sound of the needle passing over scratches and then a high, melancholy, beautiful voice filled the air:

Blow the wind southerly, southerly, southerly,
Blow the wind south o'er the bonnie blue sea.

Dr Ojebande lit two more enormous candles. They smelled like moss and cast long, creepy shadows. My eyes were still trying to get used to the light.

Dr Ojebande seated himself in one of the wooden chairs – the largest, with arms upholstered in dark-red velvet and a high back. There was an ancient floor-to-ceiling mirror next to him, in what looked like an ivory or bone frame.

I looked up at the ceiling. There were scraps of paper hanging from it, old and yellowing, along with what looked like bunches of herbs of some sort. Dr Ojebande looked into the fire and although it must have been my imagination, it seemed to flare up in response to his gaze.

Hanging on a coat hook were a pair of steel goggles. I couldn't imagine what Dr Ojebande would want those for. There were two huge old spears leaning against a closed door, and on another wall were three African tribal masks. One was black, the size of two heads fused together, with rows of teeth and white slit eyes and two massive horns poking out the top. Another was round, orange like a pumpkin, with round eyes and a round mouth. It reminded me of that weird painting, *The Scream* by Edvard Munch.

The third mask was the weirdest of all. It was shaped more like a potato than a head. It was massive and scarred with white markings in zigzags emanating from the centre. The eyes stared like they could see me. The mouth frowned as if it disapproved. The eyebrows pointed downwards angrily. It was a face full of hate.

I became aware of shapes moving around my feet. *Cats.* Not one or two, but a dozen of them. They were like a sea of fur. None of them seemed to register my presence, although one briefly rubbed against my leg, purring, before curling up in front of the fire.

I noticed other items on a shelf over the fireplace – old-fashioned ceramic bottles with labels on them. One read "Hair". Another read "Nails". A third read "Urine". Above the shelf there was a five-pointed star held within a circle containing four Hebrew letters, a design that I knew was called a "Tetragrammaton". It represented the biblical God, Yahweh, the Hebrew divinity of the Old Testament. There was also what seemed to be a mirror – but it was completely black.

Dr Ojebande rose from his chair and went to a small kitchen that adjoined the main room. He came back holding a glass of frothing, bubbling liquid. It was so effervescent that the glass was overflowing. In the firelight it appeared a sickly orange. I assumed that it must be a potion of some sort. He stared at the glass for a few seconds, watching the bubbles subside, then knocked most of it back in one go.

I wanted to get out of there as quickly as possible.

Bloody well beam me bloody up, Scotty.

I had known that Dr Ojebande was peculiar, but I'd never thought that he was *this* weird. Dr Ojebande, meanwhile, was now sitting with his eyes closed on the straight-backed chair. He was sitting bolt upright, unmoving. He had not changed out of the black suit he wore, or the heavy shoes.

The song continued:

> *Blow the wind southerly, southerly, southerly,*
> *Blow, bonnie breeze, my lover to me.*

Treading as softly as I could, I started to walk back towards the door of the house, keeping my eyes on Dr Ojebande at all times, when, to my horror, his eyes flickered open and he stared right at me. I knew he couldn't see me, but it felt as if I were illuminated in a spotlight.

> *They told me last night there were ships in the offing,*
> *And I hurried down to the deep rolling sea;*
> *But my eye could not see it wherever might be it,*
> *The barque that is bearing my lover to me.*

My desire to get out of there redoubled. It was like being in that room with Mr Maurice Bailey the bus driver, but much, much worse. I kept walking.

Then that bird started cawing again: "Beware. Beware. Beware."

I didn't care if it was really speaking or not. It was freaking me out. I almost broke into a run for the door.

A cat was blocking my way. I tried to inch past it, but it suddenly raked its claws viciously across my ankle.

I gasped in pain, then suppressed it. All the same, Dr Ojebande's head whipped round to look in my direction.

I was just reaching for the door handle when, for the first time, Dr Ojebande spoke. His voice was low and sonorous, as if he was praying. I could just about make the words out. They sent a chill down my spine.

"'Everything is space, within and without. The mirror is a wall that reflects all your doubt.'"

I stared back at Dr Ojebande in a state of panic. Then I shifted my gaze to the full-length mirror on the wall to his right.

It showed my reflection plainly. I looked cold, wet and very scared. There was a large rip at the bottom of my trousers where the barbed wire had torn them.

I had been discovered. The spell was broken.

Dr Ojebande was smiling. I wanted to run, but I couldn't. My feet felt rooted to the spot.

"Beware. Beware. Beware."

My terrified eyes turned to where the sound was coming from. In the gloom in the corner of the room I saw an enormous birdcage. The black bird was sitting on a perch inside it, squawking. The door to the cage was open.

The music stopped, and the bird grew quiet. There was a long silence, with Dr Ojebande sitting on his chair and me standing, mid-stride, on my way to the door.

Dr Ojebande spoke first. He nodded towards the bird.

"He's trying to warn me, not you."

"Beware. Beware. Beware," said the bird again.

Dr Ojebande waved a hand in its direction, and it fell silent.

"Why don't you sit down, Nyman?"

His voice was not steely and authoritative like it was in the classroom. It was, to my surprise, pleasant and warm, even welcoming.

"Don't be afraid, Strato. There's nothing to be afraid of here."

I remained standing. I heard my voice creaking out of my throat, as if it was being forcibly dragged through the air.

"How…?"

My voice dried up, but Dr Ojebande answered anyway.

"I had a strong instinct I was being followed. I knew that whatever it was would reveal itself once it got inside the house. The forces in here are too potent to resist."

Dr Ojebande shrugged, still smiling. Then he spoke, in a low, hypnotic monotone:

"'A warning must be clearly took
By those that wish to use this book.
Do not be seen, or discovered, or let
The secret be known lest thy power be forfeit.'"

He looked up again.

"How do you know about the book?" I stuttered. My voice was as fragile as a leaf skeleton.

"I did some research."

I looked up nervously at the masks on the wall.

Dr Ojebande followed my gaze and then started laughing uproariously. He didn't stop for about a minute. Then he indicated for me to sit down in the chair next to him.

"Those are souvenirs from a beach holiday I took in Mombasa a few years ago. They're all fakes. I bought them from a hawker. I was cheated, of course. Paid three times what they were worth."

I still didn't move. I decided to risk another question.

"So you're not some kind of—"

Dr Ojebande interrupted before I could finish.

"*Sangoma*? African witch doctor? I am no more a sangoma than you are. Less. My family has been in this part of the country for twenty generations. I am British, Strato, just as you are. Now, enough of this silly talk. Would you like a glass of lemonade or something?"

Dr Ojebande swallowed the seething, bubbling drink I had seen him carry in from the kitchen.

"What … what was that?" I asked.

"Andrews Liver Salts," he replied blithely. "For indigestion. I suffer from it terribly. Bad diet, I'm afraid. Too many ready meals. Sit down, sit down."

I was tentatively moving towards the chair when something made me jump half out of my skin. A small white shape darted across the floor, only to disappear on the other side of the room. I froze again, but Dr Ojebande just started laughing again.

"It's only a mouse. A pet I keep. I call him 'Old Familiar'. He has a few friends around here too. Cats like him. Don't be nervous. He's perfectly friendly and perfectly clean. Now, what about that drink?"

Not knowing what else to do, I sat down. Dr Ojebande disappeared into the kitchen and returned with a cup of tea for himself and a glass of lemonade for me. On the glass was a picture of Mickey Mouse.

"It's a bit childish, but it's the only one I have. I keep it for when my nephew comes to visit. He's five."

He also held out a Curly Wurly bar.

"I know you like them. I've seen them in your lunchbox. So I picked some up from the supermarket a while ago."

"But how did you know…?"

He shrugged. "I didn't. Not for sure. But it's best to be prepared for visitors."

Dr Ojebande settled down in the chair next to me and regarded me mildly. My feelings of anxiety were slowly dissipating, but I still felt that I was in a very weird situation. I sipped at the lemonade. The little Mickey Mouse picture somehow made me feel better, more at ease. My throat felt slightly less parched.

A black-and-white cat – the one that had scratched me – came and sat on Dr Ojebande's lap and started purring. Dr Ojebande stroked him with a single, bony finger.

"What were you doing following me home?" he said quietly. "I would call that a violation of privacy, wouldn't you?"

I nodded, feeling suddenly ashamed.

"After all, if you are given a very special power, using it simply to satisfy idle curiosity is rather abusing that power, don't you think?"

Dr Ojebande seemed entirely matter-of-fact about this, as if thirteen-year-old boys with the power to be invisible were the most commonplace things in the world.

"Anyway, why on earth would you want to follow me

home? I'm not so interesting, am I? Just a dry, dusty old Tartar of a teacher."

A "Tartar", incidentally, is "someone who is unduly harsh or fierce".

"I don't know," I mumbled. "I just saw you walking home and felt an … impulse to follow you. I don't know what I was expecting to find out."

"It was probably the grimoire," said Dr Ojebande. "It almost certainly picked up the energy coming from me and led you in my direction."

"What's a grimoire?"

"The spell book. Do you have it with you?"

I fumbled in my bag. It wasn't there. I emptied the bag on the stone floor: exercise books, sweets, a compass, a comic, tissues, a few stickers. No book.

"But I know that I put it in..."

"It's gone," said Dr Ojebande, mildly. "As soon as I realized what you were – what you had become – it returned to wherever it came from. You knew that when someone found out you were invisible, the power would disappear? The book went with it."

I felt sad – but somehow not sad at the same time. Being invisible had been good fun, but it had been hard, too. The truth wasn't as great as everybody said it was. I thought I now understood a little more why grown-ups lied so much.

"How did you come by it?" asked Dr Ojebande, sipping at his cup of tea. "Although I think I can guess."

"I got it from the bookshop where you got the—"

I stopped myself, too late. For the first time, Dr Ojebande seemed surprised.

"Go on," he said.

"Where you got the book about witchcraft," I said, looking at my feet.

A look of understanding came over his face. "So you followed me there, too. And that was *you* making that ridiculous quacking noise in the old church."

"Yes."

"You'd make a good private eye. I didn't know I was being followed. I thought that noise came from some kind of mischievous spirit playing a trick on me."

"What were you doing there? In that old church."

Mr Ojebande looked at me as if I was an idiot. "What do people usually do in a church?"

"Pray."

"Exactly."

"But why would you pray with a book about witchcraft?"

"I wish you showed this much curiosity at school."

"School isn't so interesting."

Mr Ojebande sighed.

"The book is not a book of witchcraft. It is a book disproving witchcraft. Reginald Scot, the writer, thought it didn't exist and set out to destroy the myth. The book is full of spells and conjuring tricks and incantations. Most of them, as the writer suggested, are nonsense. But not all of them. Mixed in with all the fakery and flummery are words that have real power, verses that are enchantments. Or so I believe. The late Mr Scot would no doubt disagree with me."

"So it is witchcraft…?"

"You can call it that. I wouldn't. On the contrary. The

cunning folk stand *against* black magic, on the side of good. We've always fought against the demons, the spirits, the faeries, the old ways. It's cost us dearly, but the battle is more or less won. That old, dark world of witches and monsters has almost passed away. Those few of us who are left just indulge in a bit of casual do-gooding nowadays. Keep moving about, helping where we can."

"Who are the cunning folk?" My head suddenly felt like it was about to short-circuit. Who was Dr Ojebande? How could my physics teacher be sitting there talking about all this weirdness, so completely unperturbed?

"The *dyn hysbys*, the pellars, the wise men and women," said Dr Ojebande, matter-of-factly. "'Cunnan' means 'to know'. We are people who know. Nowadays, scientists are the cunning folk, but once it was different. We go way back. Mostly forgotten now. Just a few old families left."

Dr Ojebande took another sip of tea and told me more about the cunning folk – how they had existed since medieval times, how they had sometimes used sorcery to achieve their ends – herbs, potions, prayers, spells. Some of them had been Christians who fought against black magic, others were simply people with a "special talent" that they used for good. Some were gypsies, and a few, like Dr Ojebande, managed to live something like a normal life.

"But most of that has gone now," said Dr Ojebande. "Science holds all the cards nowadays. It thinks it knows everything."

"But it doesn't," I said.

"That's right," said Dr Ojebande. He looked pointedly

at his watch. "Now then, what time is it? I really ought to be—"

"If you were praying, what were you praying for?" I asked.

Dr Ojebande grinned. I noticed that his back teeth glinted with gold caps.

"You're a very nosy young man. If you must know, I was praying for young Mr Turnbull – I could tell that he needed help. I find that people who cause others to suffer are usually suffering themselves. And you know what?"

"What?"

"I think the prayer worked. Thanks to you."

He gave me a kind smile, and then looked at his watch again. Clearly he had better things to do than chat with an invisible boy. Or an ex-invisible boy. But I was rooted there – I was desperate to find out more.

"Did you get the book on witchcraft from the man with the ginger moustache?" I asked

"Ah, Old Berewold," said Dr Ojebande ruminatively. "Is that who gave you the grimoire? Not a bad old chap, in his way, for a *dyn hysbys*. Do you know he's one hundred and seven years old? You wouldn't think it, would you? Anyway, he's not the sharpest tool in the box. Doesn't always think things through. Smells bad too. Like liver and onions. Did you notice that?"

I shook my head. Dr Ojebande continued.

"Don't know that it was very sensible to put a grimoire into the hands of a troubled thirteen-year-old boy, however clever that boy happens to be. Still, folk like us aren't always wise, even though our intentions are usually good. Now then, what do you think? Of your experience, I mean."

He looked at me, with his eyes no longer lazy but piercing and bright.

"I don't know," I said honestly. "It's been painful. But I think it's helped me, in a strange way."

"Good," said Dr Ojebande. "I'm pleased. Though you really never know for sure, do you?"

I drained my glass of lemonade. The pervading sense of weirdness was wearing off. I was vaguely relieved to be rid of my "gift". It felt as if it might have become addictive.

Talking to Dr Ojebande now was more like talking to a friendly uncle than to a teacher or some kind of warlock. Without really thinking, I blurted out some of my own mysteries. How I needed to know how to kiss Susan Brown, how to save Peaches' and Melchior's relationship, and how to deal with Mr Maurice Bailey – how I needed to sort everything out somehow, and how I wished magic could help me.

Dr Ojebande stared deeply into the fire for ten seconds, and then he looked at me.

"If I have any advice for you, it comes down to this: never imagine you know more than you do. Because the truth is, you almost certainly know less than you think."

I nodded. Dr Ojebande continued.

"I don't know about answers, though. But it's OK not to know. If we knew everything, it would be dreadful. Life is all about mysteries. People who try to kill mysteries try to kill life. Fortunately, life is so strange we are unlikely ever to run out of them. As my great-great-grandfather used to say, 'It's amazing the number of things there are that ain't.'"

"But what about my parents?"

Dr Ojebande shook his head sadly. "There's no help for those kinds of things. Your mother and father will just have to sort it out themselves. Maybe everything will work out. I have a good feeling about it, for what it's worth. As for Susan Brown, you don't need magic – you just need courage. Maybe she'll reject you. So what? There will be other girls. It's the price you pay for trying. As for Maurice Bailey – well, I do have an idea about that. Nothing magical though."

He told me his idea – and it was a pretty good one, I had to admit.

Then I said, "Is 'Ojebande' even your real name?"

"No," he said. "My real name is a secret. And don't ask. You wouldn't be able to pronounce it."

After I had been there for what seemed like hours, I realized I should go home. Almost reluctantly now, I rose to leave.

"You're going," said Dr Ojebande. It wasn't a question, but a statement.

"My mother will be getting worried," I said. "But to tell you the truth, I'm a bit afraid of that bull in the field on the way home."

"He won't give you any trouble. He's gone to sleep now."

"How do you know?"

"A little bird told me."

He turned his gaze to the window. There, framed against the darkness, was the black bird with the white mark on its wing. It had left its cage and somehow made its way outside. The bird opened its beak once, let out a caw and flew away.

I turned back to Dr Ojebande. He handed me a big torch and draped an old blanket over my shoulders. Then he gave me the rest of the Curly Wurlys.

"I don't really like them," he said. "You might as well finish them off."

"Thank you, Dr Ojebande," I said.

"You're welcome," he replied.

"I'm not sure how I'm going to be able to talk to you next term," I said.

Dr Ojebande – or whatever his real name was – looked sad.

"You won't have to," he said. "I'm moving on."

"You're leaving?" I was shocked.

"Yes. We cunning folk never stay too long in one place. It doesn't do. Scientists might find us and cut us open to learn what makes us tick. So this was the last day of my last term."

He smiled and reached a hand out to me.

"Have a happy Christmas, Strato," he said, shaking my hand.

"You too, Dr Ojebande," I said.

And then I walked out of the door, unafraid, into the darkness.

CHAPTER SEVENTEEN

OUT OF THE SHADOW OF NONAGE

So that's how I lost my power of invisibility. Perhaps it was my fault for snooping once too often.

Without my special gift, I could no longer eavesdrop in order to work out what the Big Gesture might be – the gesture that Melchior needed to make in order to win Peaches back.

I had more or less given up on the two of them anyway. Admittedly their arguments had become less frequent, but I imagined that was simply because Melchior wasn't there all the time. He still came around to the house often enough – I thought they were both being quite mature about the break-up, actually. Sometimes they had meals together, or even watched the TV side by side, before Melchior returned to his small, dingy hotel room with the sad chocolate on the pillow.

I dreaded Christmas Day as it loomed ahead of us. All the normal families were going to be gathering happily by the tree. But for me, this Christmas would simply be the first of many when we were separate instead of together.

Even if we were all in the same room, we would be separate.

So I had a sense of deep foreboding when, a few days after the school holidays started, Melchior and Peaches called me down to the front room for an "important talk".

It was a Tuesday and Melchior had come home and cooked – or should I say overcooked? – a roast chicken for us. After lunch, I had gone back up to my room to watch TV and the two of them had stayed together in the front room talking to one another in hushed tones – too hushed for me to work out what they were saying by lurking outside the door. A few days earlier that wouldn't have mattered, but now I had no way of knowing what was going on.

I was pretty sure I knew what was coming, though. Melchior had clearly failed to come up with the Big Gesture and Peaches had got tired of waiting. I felt very, very sad, and wished that I could be invisible once more so that no one could ever see me again as long as I lived – so that I could be like the air, or nothing at all.

I sat down with a heart that felt like it was made of osmium or iridim, or some other heavy metal. I thought for a moment I was going to cry, and I never cry. Peaches and Melchior looked at me as if they were deeply concerned. They stared at me gravely, seated on either side of the table.

Peaches spoke first. Her voice was softer than usual, and she glanced across to Melchior from time to time, as if seeking reassurance.

"We know you've had a hard time of it lately," she

said. "We know it hasn't been easy for you. And we're both very, very sorry."

Melchior nodded. I said nothing and waited for the bombshell to drop once all the bloody flim-flam was out of the way.

"We haven't thought about you enough," continued Peaches. "We've only thought about ourselves. Me and my book, and your father and his job and … what happened in London between him and—"

Melchior interrupted.

"Suffice to say, that time is now over. Today we are going to begin a new phase of our lives. An exciting new phase."

I was no fool – not any more. I had learned a bit over the last few weeks. I had found out, under experimental conditions, how adults behaved. "An exciting new phase" meant that a disaster was coming. I knew that in politics this is called "spin", but I preferred to give it its real name – lies. They wanted to break the news to me now so that we wouldn't all have to act out a complete lie of family happiness together on Christmas Day. They were splitting up once and for all. It was all over.

I looked at Peaches and noticed that she was crying. This was awful. I just wanted to get out of there. But I kept myself fixed to the chair and stared at a spot on the wall as if it was the most fascinating thing I had ever seen.

"You see, the thing is," continued Melchior, "your mother and I—"

"I'm not a *complete* bloody idiot," I snapped.

I was amazed at how loud my voice was – loud and bitter.

"Calm down," said Peaches, wiping her eyes and reaching to touch my arm.

I shrugged her off.

"Don't tell me to calm down. You're going to be apart *for good*. I know all about it. You didn't even have the … decency to wait until after Christmas. Nice present, Santa! Thanks a lot. Oh yeah, I forgot. There isn't any Santa. That was just another one of your stories."

My eyes stinging, I turned and ran up to my room, slamming the door behind me. I would have locked it. But I didn't have a key. Or a lock, for that matter.

Once I was in there I just wanted to throw myself at the mirror again, and smash it to pieces – smash myself to pieces. I knew I wouldn't turn invisible this time. I would be all too solid, flesh and blood. But maybe physical pain would be some kind of escape from what I was feeling.

So that's exactly what I did. I fixed the mirror with a stare, then without allowing another thought to enter my head, I ran at it, full pelt, head first.

This time – of course – I didn't disappear into the other side of the glass. I smashed into it, and it shattered with a deafening crash. A piece of glass cut my arm and it began to bleed. Shards of mirror scattered all over the floor. I stamped on them with my shoe, breaking them into smaller pieces.

Still I didn't cry.

At that point, my parents both rushed into the room.

"Strato. Strato!"

"GO AWAY!" I yelled. "What do you WANT?"

I had never heard myself talk so wildly.

Peaches saw the blood on my arm. It was only a tiny cut, but she started making an awful fuss.

"Oh! You've hurt yourself. My poor Strato!"

She rushed up and put her arms around me, then got a tissue from my desk and dabbed at the small, red stain. I let myself be held. Meanwhile, Melchior started picking up the glass from the floor. I shrugged Peaches off and wiped my eyes dry with the back of my sleeve.

"I'm fine. Can you both leave me on my own, please. I want to be by myself."

I sat down on the bed, crossing my arms, my mouth fixed in a grimace. Melchior had stopped picking up pieces of glass and went to stand next to Peaches. To my surprise, he took her hand. For some reason, they both started smiling, which infuriated me even more. I was just considering throwing something at them when Melchior finally spoke.

"We're not splitting up, Strato."

"Of course you're splitting up," I said. "You've already split up. Just have the guts to tell me the truth for once."

"We're not splitting up – really," said Peaches.

At this point, Melchior held out my mother's left hand for me to see. On her fourth finger was a ring I had never seen before, with a sparkling jewel that I presumed to be a diamond on it.

"So you bought her a new ring. So what?"

"It's an engagement ring, Strato," said Melchior quietly.

"A *what?*" I said, not really understanding.

"An engagement ring. Marie-France has agreed to be my wife."

I rocked back in astonishment. Was this some new joke, some freshly-minted falsehood? I looked at Peaches fiercely.

She nodded silently, in confirmation. Then she said, "It's true, Strato. Yesterday, your father asked me to marry him. Today, I said yes. Even though he doesn't know how to cook a chicken properly."

They both laughed.

"We're getting married on Saturday, Strato. In four days' time," said Melchior.

"But that's Christmas Eve."

"There's no law against getting married on Christmas Eve, you know," said Peaches. "And then we can start our first day of married life on Christmas Day."

I was entirely lost for words.

"What's gone is gone, Strato," said Peaches. "Forgiveness is tough, very tough indeed, but I think – finally – I've found a way to get to it. I've swallowed my pride and I've swallowed my hurt. Perhaps one day you'll manage it too. Perhaps one day you'll forgive me and your father for all that we've put you through."

I said nothing. I was still in a sulk, although the grounds of my sulking had fallen away from under me.

"I'm very happy," said Melchior. "We're both very happy, Strato. Things are going to be OK. I'm sure of it, somehow."

"How do you know?" I said, trying to hold on to my anger. But it had almost entirely dissipated.

"Call it instinct," said Peaches.

"It just makes sense," said Melchior.

"It wasn't right for me to write the book – with or without your permission," said Peaches, the ring flashing on her finger. "I've shelved it."

"Won't you have to pay the advance back?" I muttered, still not quite believing what I was hearing.

Melchior and Peaches exchanged glances.

"How did you know about that?" said Peaches suspiciously.

I didn't say anything.

Peaches decided to let it go.

"The thing is, I've started a new book – a novel this time – about moving from a London suburb to a weird little village in the country. It's what everybody dreams of – to move to the country and become a novelist. It's called *The Grass Is Greener*. Nothing about geeks. My publishers like it – they really like it, Strato. So I don't have to pay the advance back, so long as I give them this book instead."

"So *Welcome to the Geek Squad* is…"

"In the bottom drawer – for the time being at least. Perhaps when you are older you will look at it and feel differently about it. Maybe you'll want it out there, in which case we'll think about it again. But whatever happens, it will get a new title. Apart from anything else, you're not a geek."

"What am I then?"

"You're simply the most interesting boy I know."

Melchior nodded. "I agree. One hundred per cent."

Then they both came across to my bed where I was sitting and hugged me. Finally believing that they were actually telling the truth – for once – I hugged them back.

Then I did something I almost never do. I began to cry – tears of joy and relief. I couldn't stop. It was only water and salt and a few trace elements, but it changed me somehow. When I'd finished, I somehow felt solid again, more *there* than I had been before, if you can understand that.

I felt so full of love then, and I wondered what science had to say about love. And of course, it had nothing at all to say. Because love is just another kind of magic. You can't see it and you can't touch it but it is the most important thing in the world, perhaps the entire known universe.

Then we all went to Mr Milkee's in the town centre and had huge bowls of ice cream. I had a selection of brown – chestnut, hazelnut, toffee and cappuccino – and it was magnificent. But better still, Melchior and Peaches held hands as I made my way through every scoop.

Adults, despite all their flaws, can be very cute.

But Melchior and Peaches had one final surprise for me – as if I hadn't had enough shocks for one day.

"Strato. Can we ask you something?" said Melchior, as I was finishing my last spoonful of ice cream. "It's all right if you say no. And I realize it will be difficult for you. Given your temperament."

"You see, it's like this," said Peaches. "Do you know what a 'best man' is?"

"Of course," I said, not quite getting it. "He holds the ring and makes speeches and stuff."

They smiled.

"Well – we were hoping that you might be our best man," said Peaches.

"We'd be very honoured," said Melchior.

I swear I felt a cold sweat break out on my forehead.

"You mean you want me to make a *speech*? In front of *people*? On my *own*?"

The terror must have come through in my voice, because Peaches turned to Melchior.

"I told you it was too much to ask," she said, patting the back of his hand with hers.

"I know. It was a crazy idea. Don't worry about it, Strato," said Melchior, turning to me. "We can always find someone who will—"

"I'll do it," I said.

"What?" they said in unison.

"I'll do it," I repeated. "Somehow, I'll do it."

Peaches and Melchior smiled.

I was glad they were happy. Because I felt that I'd just been sentenced to a fate worse than death.

CHAPTER EIGHTEEN

THE GREAT TERROR

The wedding took place at 2.00 p.m. in a fifteenth-century church in the town centre. To my amazement, about fifty of Melchior's and Peaches' friends had come down from London to join in the ceremony.

I was dressed in a brand-new suit – ice blue, with sharp, narrow lapels. I'd had a haircut, and I'd even had a shave – the first one ever, but there had definitely been stubble appearing on my top lip and it made me look dirty so I razored it off.

I watched the people walk into the church and turned the ring in my pocket round and round with my finger. A lot of the guests told me, as I greeted them at the entrance to the church, that I had grown up suddenly. I felt in some strange way that they were right.

My father, dressed in a pale-grey suit with a rose in his buttonhole, waited at the altar for my mother to arrive, while I stood at the door, shifting from foot to foot. Since Peaches' father was long dead, I was giving her away as well as being best man. I looked into the church. I could see Susan Brown, dressed in a plain dark-green dress, sitting off to the left. She was the only person of my age there, and I was very glad that she had come. I caught her eye, and she gave me a quiet smile. It made me feel a bit stronger, but I was still weak at the knees.

I felt in my left-hand pocket, where there was a piece of paper. My speech was written on it, and every time I thought of standing up in front of fifty people and speaking it out loud it made the hair on the back of my neck stand up. Going into Dr Ojebande's house had been a stroll in the park in comparison.

I watched as an old dark-blue Morris Traveller, with its wooden beams and friendly snub face, turned into the end of the street and moved towards the church. It was polished to a bright sheen, and stretched out over the bonnet were two white ribbons.

The car pulled up in front of the church and Peaches climbed out. She looked incredible. Her dress was cream rather than white, and it looked antique, with delicate bits of lace frilling everywhere. She was wearing a veil, but I could see her face behind it. It looked beatific.

"Beatific", incidentally, means "blissful" or "serene".

She smiled at me, and I smiled back. Then the organ started up, she took my arm and step by slow step we made our way down the aisle. When we reached the altar where the vicar was waiting to perform the ceremony, I saw Melchior turn to look at her. His face was a picture. It was as if his features melted. He didn't smile exactly. It was more as if he was awestruck. He reached out and touched the veil with the tip of his finger, just as he used to touch my face. Then he turned to the vicar and the ceremony began.

Twenty-two minutes later, my mother and father were

married. I didn't fumble or drop the ring. Nobody stood up to say that they objected to the two of them being married, not even Dorothea Beckwith-Hinds, whose dress was exquisitely awful. She looked like she had fallen into a giant yellow meringue and been unable to extricate herself.

The vicar pronounced them man and wife, and the whole congregation burst into applause as Melchior kissed his bride. When the clapping began to die down, one person just kept going, unable to stop.

But eventually Susan Brown shot me a friendly glance, and I put my hands in my pockets.

About three hours later the moment I had been dreading came. No wonder public speaking was the thing that people feared most in the world. But I was determined to do it for my parents.

We were in a room above an old pub, and I was sitting to the right of Melchior and Peaches. Thoughtfully, knowing how quiet my voice was, Melchior had set up a microphone for me. The guests had all finished their puddings and were looking towards our table, waiting for the speeches to begin. I had fidgeted with my piece of paper so much that it felt like a lump of putty in my pocket. I took the paper out and stared at it. It was so screwed up and sweaty I could barely read it.

I decided I couldn't put it off any longer. I stood up.

I started to tap my wine glass with a spoon as my father had told me to do, to signal the beginning of the speeches.

Instead of a clear ringing tone, there was a shattering

tinkle. The glass broke. The Coca-Cola that I had filled my wine glass with spilled onto the white tablecloth, leaving a spreading dark stain.

Immediately, to my consternation, the room fell silent. I looked down at Peaches and Melchior, who were staring up at me expectantly. As was every single person in the room.

Nobody laughed at the fact that I had just broken the glass, which made me doubly nervous.

I glanced across at Susan Brown. She looked as anxious as I felt. I could tell that she was having doubts about whether I was going to be able to carry this off.

I picked up the microphone, switched it on and tapped it, hoping that the sheen of sweat on my finger wouldn't mean I would be electrocuted.

Nothing happened.

I tapped it again. The mic was dead.

The silence had grown deeper. If it went on much longer, awkwardness and embarrassment were going to creep into the room like uninvited guests.

My mind went blank. A wave of pure panic swept over me. The words on the piece of paper swam in front of my eyes. I looked desperately around the room for inspiration, but there were just eyes, eyes, dozens of eyes, all trained on me and waiting for me to make a fool of myself.

I gulped. More seconds passed. Susan Brown shifted uncomfortably in her seat. I glanced down at Melchior and Peaches. Their grins were beginning to look a bit starched into place.

I looked over to the window, now wishing that the

ground would swallow me entirely. My throat burned, a dry heat.

I saw a black shape in the window. I squinted, and focused.

It was a bird.

It was Dr Ojebande's bird.

It looked at me, and then I swear it did something impossible.

It winked.

And at that moment, for some reason, my face stretched into a broad smile and the spell broke. Putting down my microphone and casting aside my piece of paper with the speech written on it, I turned to the crowd and spoke, in a loud, clear voice.

"There's a thing I read about in science called quantum entanglement."

Out of the corner of my eye, I could see my father putting his head into his hands. He clearly thought I had lost my mojo completely. Not that I had any mojo to lose. He knew that I wasn't following the speech I'd written.

I wasn't saying any of the stuff on the piece of paper – welcoming the guests, thanking them for coming, telling a few jokes etc. This was completely different. The words were just arriving in my head as I stood there.

Among the faces in the crowd there was simply puzzlement and anxiety.

I pressed on, my voice still loud and clear.

"It's very hard to explain, but the thing is, two particles are sometimes so closely entangled that if one of them changes, the other one changes too. So if you had two photons … or … well, you know, if a nucleus ejects two particles, they must have opposite spin … one spins clockwise and one spins anticlockwise…"

I could sense a deepening unease in the crowd. I was losing them and I had hardly even started. I looked up for my friend, the bird. It had disappeared. I was on my own.

When I started speaking again, I could hear my own voice faltering slightly.

"Forget about the photons. It doesn't matter what you call them."

It occurred to me, with astonishment, that I was no longer shy – not today, anyway. The fear had gone. I didn't know where it had gone, but it had.

I felt my voice growing stronger again.

"The thing is, these two tiny things are so tangled together, that if you separate them and put them millions or even billions of miles apart, they still know about each other. They still *relate* to each other.

"If one of them changes, the other one changes – immediately, in the same millisecond. They each know what is happening to the other one, even though they may be light years apart. That's how intimate they are. That's how entwined their destinies are."

I paused. A lot of furrowed brows. My father still had his head in his hands.

"I think that this is like love. I feel that two people who really love one another are connected that closely. Peaches and Melchior are connected that closely. How-ever far they drift away, they are always right there with each other, even if sometimes they seem far apart.

"If one changes, the other one changes. Just like two particles. They know each other. They *are* each other. They are entangled, forever together. That's what marriage is. Isn't it?"

I stared above the heads of the people in front of me, afraid to look in their faces for what I might see there.

"I am entangled too. We are all entangled. Forever together. Wherever we travel, and whatever we are when we're apart. That's what love is, I suppose. Isn't it? Whatever happens to them, happens to me. And what has happened to them today makes me the happiest particle in the universe."

My voice faded away. Complete silence. I didn't know whether I had lost them or won them over. My father had at least taken his head out of his hands. And my mother was about to either smile or frown.

I couldn't stretch the thing out any longer. I couldn't think of anything else to say.

So I latched on to an unbroken glass and held it up for the toast.

I was just about to say the words my father had told me to say, when I was stopped in my tracks.

Susan Brown started clapping.

Then her mother, who was sitting with her, started clapping. Then a few more people at the next table. Then a few more.

Then the whole room was clapping and cheering. It was twenty-one seconds before they were quiet enough for me to raise my glass and say what I wanted, desperately, to say. To set a seal on what would never be broken.

"Ladies and gentlemen – the bride and groom."

*

Everything changes. Everything is happening all the time, my dad always says. Even a table is happening, if you look closely enough. It's all change, and change hurts, but change is good.

After that day, things definitely changed. They got better. The arguments between Peaches and Melchior dried up completely. My parents seemed to be drawn together like two poles of an electromagnetic force. Marriage suited them. Our Christmas Day together was the best I could remember. I got a Sky-Watcher EXPLORER-130EM telescope with 130 mm f/900 Newtonian Reflector with RA motor drive. I'm sure you'll agree, that's as good as it gets.

Me, Lloyd Archibald Turnbull and Susan Brown became good friends. One of the two Waynes was excluded from school, while the other was put down a class because his marks were so bad, so we didn't really have to deal with them any more.

Lloyd Archibald Turnbull still had a difficult time with his mother – she became neurotic and terrified of ghosts after I paid her that little visit – but she pretty much stopped hitting him. He remained both pleasant and industrious – I'm sure Dr Ojebande would have been proud of him. Also, he had an operation on his arm, and after a lot of hard work and perseverance, he was able to use it again.

I never did anything about Dr Ojebande's suggestion for dealing with Mr Maurice Bailey. On the other hand, I *did* tell Lloyd Turnbull about what he'd been doing to me. And I've got a theory he did do something about it.

All I know is that a few days after I told Lloyd Turnbull, Mr Bailey's precious Land Rover suffered a fatal seizure. It wouldn't start, however much he coaxed it. And when he'd taken it to three different mechanics to try and find out what was the matter, the last one finally worked it out.

It turned out that someone had put several jars of marmalade – presumably Robertson's – into the petrol tank. Needless to say, this had not been all that healthy for the engine – to put it mildly. Fact is, Mr Bailey didn't drive his Land Rover around town after that.

I felt a little sorry for him. After all, not even Mr Bailey is all bad. I know that, because I saw him looking after the little old lady who lived next door to him. And maybe he was once just like Lloyd Turnbull – bullied by his mum or dad – and he just took all that anger out on other people.

But I didn't feel all *that* sorry for him.

After all, he was a bloody nutcase.

I did go back to the bookshop where I found *How To be Invisible* to see if I could get another copy, but when I looked, the bookshop wasn't there any more. It was now a cafe called Eatz. I suppose old Berewold, like Dr Ojebande – or whatever his real name was – had moved on, like cunning folk do.

I don't suppose I shall ever come across another cunning person, but it was a real privilege that I did. Now I am sure of what I knew all along – that science isn't the end of the story, that there are mysteries everywhere, inside science and outside.

Nobody knows all the secrets. And nobody ever will.

Things are good. I don't ask Scotty to beam me up much any more.

You may be wondering what happened with me and Susan Brown – whether I ever plucked up the courage to kiss her.

I did. It was easy after I'd made the speech. Nothing will be that hard again. I'm not going to tell you what happened after that. It's something you shouldn't know about. It's too private.

I'll say this much. For a while we went to one another's houses and chatted about physics and biology, and watched silly films together and had a great, geeky time. After she taught me to swim in the river, we went swimming there together on hot summer evenings the following year – but not the year after that. Eventually we grew apart.

I suppose back then we were both living under the shadow of nonage.

"Nonage", incidentally, is an old-fashioned word meaning "the time just before adolescence".

Now I am moving out of the shadow of nonage. And into the sunlight, which sometimes warms and sometimes burns.

So that is the story of how I learned how to be invisible. It's absolutely true, but I can't prove it. Then again, scientific proof isn't everything. But there is circumstantial evidence of a sort, because if you met me face to face, you would know that I don't have enough imagination to make this sort of thing up. All I am capable of doing is observing, and recording facts, and formulating theories. And remembering, of course. Remembering, and learning as much as I can from all I remember.

For instance, I will never forget that day when Susan Brown taught me to swim. All you had to do, she said, was trust the water, then swimming was easy.

That lesson stuck in my mind because it occurred to me that the same thing applies to people.

You have to trust people even though they let you down, and trust them again, and then again. I learned to trust that my mother and father would make things right for me and each other, and I trusted myself to trust them.

Trust is invisible too, but it turns out that it's the invisible things that matter most of all. Neutrinos, quarks, gravity, anti-matter, leptons, love, hope, dignity, courage, trust.

I may not be invisible any more, but I still live in the invisible world. We all do. It's much more important than the other one.

To quote from my favourite book, which I shall never see again, but which I think about all the time:

> *That which matters*
> *Is not of matter made.*
> *Words hide paper.*
> *Paper conceals space.*
> *All is emptiness.*
> *And all things forever*
> *From that emptiness*
> *Spring.*

ACKNOWLEDGEMENTS

I would like to thank James le Fanu, Frank Close and Michael Marten for their contributions towards my rudimentary scientific understandings.

Also thanks to Jessica Arah for her time and editorial insight and apologies to Kate Bush for stealing her title.